The Paper Girl

Copyright © 2007 Rhaina Rivers
All rights reserved.
ISBN: 1-4196-6608-8
ISBN-13: 978-1419666087

Visit www.booksurge.com to order additional copies.

The Paper Girl

Rhaina Rivers

2007

The Paper Girl

I would like to dedicate this book my children: Namely Monica, Stan, Austin, Adele, Joyce, Marissa and Mark. Also to dedicate it to my sister Gwen in Australia, and to my brother Adrian in Alberta.

Thank you to Adele and Mark for all their technical assistance.

CHAPTER ONE

It was nearly dark as Charlie limped her way through the back streets of the town, where she had lived all her life. She could see the last of the red sunset which was almost completely covered by jagged, streaky black clouds. Charlie was too tired and her feet hurt too much for her to be able to appreciate the beauties of nature. All she could think of was being able to lie down for awhile. She had been delivering papers, for what seemed to her to be hours. Charlie lived with her mother in the remains of an old burned out building on the edge of town. The owner of the building had abandoned it years ago. It was said that he had no insurance to rebuild and so he left town, and nobody had heard from him since. There was no running water or electricity, as no one was paying utilities. Charlie's mother had furnished the one downstairs room with old things that she had scavenged from other people's cast offs. That was also where she and Charlie's clothes came from. They were more rags than clothes. Charlie's mother kept her looking like a boy. She kept her hair cut short and made her wear boy's clothes. Since Charlie had always dressed that way she didn't know the difference. She was used to eating the scraps that her mother brought home. Usually what ever could be picked up from the dumpster after the restaurants had closed. Her mother had been getting her food that way for a long time. She knew exactly when they closed and was there waiting to get the leftovers before they got too stale, or a stray cat got into them. They didn't get very many vegetables in their diet this way, but there were usually burgers and fries. Her mother heated the food on an old wood stove that she had salvaged and hooked up to the old chimney. Charlie thought that most people lived that way. She had never been allowed to talk to other people, or play with other children. Her mother would have beaten her within an inch of her life if she had caught her conversing with anyone. Charlie had to walk with her head looking downwards at the ground. She had to wear a cap pulled down almost over her eyes. She usually wasn't allowed out during the day except for when she accompanied her mother to deliver papers, or when her mother took her to a garden to pull weeds.

Her mother, Olga was considered to be queer in the head, and looked the part with her raggedy attire. People felt sorry for her and gave her odd jobs that nobody else wanted. Ever since Charlie was old enough to do anything, she had to help in what ever way her mother told her. It didn't matter how tired she got or how much her back hurt, she had to persevere and do just what she was told. If Olga, wasn't satisfied, or was just in an ugly mood she would lay the strap to her when they got home. Charlie didn't know anything about a close mother, daughter relationship. She didn't know what love was. She only knew work and how to try to be invisible.

Olga and Charlie hauled water from a town pump situated not far from their place. They did their laundry in an old bathtub, and hung their clothes on ropes strung across the basement which was their main living area. Olga managed to maintain a degree of cleanliness. Of course their beds were old used beds with ragged bedding.

Charlie staggered into the house and onto her bed. She thought it was the best place on earth. She had been walking for miles pulling an old wagon and carrying a large bag of newspapers. Her mother had been doing the same, but she had a different route. Olga had trained Charlie to handle her route and then Olga had gotten a different route for herself. Charlie was used to the walking, but she wasn't used to handling so many papers by herself. The papers had to be delivered within a certain time span, or people would complain, and that meant that Olga wouldn't get paid for all the deliveries.

Olga managed to make enough money to buy milk and eggs occasionally, or a band-aid for blistered heels. Her income wasn't supplemented by social assistance as Olga didn't know such a thing existed. She kept to herself and didn't want to know much about what was going on with the rest of society. She regarded most people as being dishonest and evil. She managed to get as much work as she could without too much contact with other people, and that satisfied her.

In the summer she looked after pulling weeds for a market garden. Charlie had to pull weeds all day no matter how tired she got, or how much she ached.

Charlie fell asleep. She was wakened by her mother yelling at her to get her lazy bones up for supper. Why didn't she have the fire started? Olga had some food salvaged from one of the restaurants. It was a carton of pancakes and waffles that had been left over. At least they were in a clean container. Of course there was no syrup. But Olga had a small bag of sugar in her so called cupboard. She reheated the pancakes on the stove and they sprinkled sugar on them. Charlie was so hungry that she thought that it was a wonderful meal. She couldn't think of it as a feast because she didn't know what a feast was. It didn't take long before they were both in bed, following their meal. They had another early morning route, which lasted for two hours. Olga didn't want Charlie out in public view late in the morning. So far no one had said that Charlie should be in school. Charlie was small and skinny for her age, but she was fourteen years old and would soon be noticed as a child who should be in school during the day.

Olga had taught Charlie some mathematics as it was necessary to be able to read numbers if one was delivering papers door to door. She had also taught Charlie how to read.

Charlie's ability to read was not very extensive. And what she read did not have the same significance to her as it would have, had she lived a normal life. Charlie had been trained to disregard most of the activities going on around her. She was locked into her and Olga's world.

A few evenings later, following her pancake supper, Charlie was returning home from delivering her share of newspapers. She noticed the figure of a man appeared several times a ways behind her. Charlie never took exactly the same way home. She had learned this from Olga as being a good way to avoid other people. So Charlie came to the conclusion that someone was following her. Charlie had a good knowledge of places one might hide, and so she hid out inside a wrecked shed, and watched through the cracks in the boards. After a few moments she heard footsteps approaching, and soon she saw a man's figure appeared hurrying along the alley. It was fairly dark out, and Charlie couldn't tell for sure if it was the same man. Charlie could feel the knots in her stomach, and she started to perspire with fear. She waited a few minutes and then cautiously took a different route home, always looking behind her to see if anyone was following.

By the time she got home she was a nervous wreck. Home never looked better to her or as comforting.

Because of Charlie's caution in getting home, Olga had arrived ahead of her. Olga immediately started in on her about why she was so late, and about how she had better get home on time after this. She went on to tell her what a lazy ungrateful brat she was. Didn't she care how hard Olga worked to provide for her? Olga was working herself into a rage. Charlie went to her bedroom to get away from Olga's accusations. This didn't please Olga, so she came after Charlie and threatened to give her a beating if she didn't get back to the kitchen. Olga had brought home their supper as usual and expected Charlie to appreciate this, and to eat it. So Charlie sat down and started to eat without saying a word until she sensed that Olga, who ate like a hungry wolf, had calmed down a little bit. Then Charlie hesitantly told her about the man she had glimpsed several times following behind her. Olga told her that it was probably her imagination working overtime. So Charlie didn't say anymore, although they both knew that Charlie had a problem. Olga had in the past considered that just such an occurrence was a distinct possibility, and so she was prepared for it. She of course hadn't taken Charlie into her confidence. A few weeks prior to this incident, Olga had applied for a different job. She had an uneasy feeling about the delivering of the newspapers. She felt that it put Charlie out in public too much, especially now that she was getting older.

So the next day after Olga was finished delivering her early morning newspapers, she followed up on the new job. She went to see the manager of the orphanage and hostel located a mile away. There was an opening for someone to do some janitor work, such as cleaning the floors, and whatever else needed cleaning up. So Olga was given the job with the understanding that her son would be helping her. Of course Olga planned on having Charlie do the actual work, as Olga didn't want to give up her own paper routes. So she cancelled Charlie's route following her trip to the orphanage. The change also meant that Charlie would be making considerably more wages, although Olga had no intention of telling Charlie that. As the evening passed Charlie's nerves settled and she looked forward to her new job of inside work instead of being exposed to the elements.

The next day on her way home from delivering papers, Charlie was on the look out for anyone following her. Sure enough as it started to get dark, Charlie caught glimpses of what looked like the same person following a ways behind her. Charlie wondered what she should do. There had to be something she could do to get away from him, but what?

Olga had instead of looking for food gone over to Charlie's likely route home. Olga stood around at a point she knew that Charlie would pass. Olga stayed out of sight until Charlie, who kept glancing behind her, had passed. Then Olga waited a little longer until a man came along, glancing around, as he was furtively sneaking along. Olga thought that she had seen him before when she was out looking for food. He seemed to be better dressed than usual, but he was the same build and height as "Wild Willy." She knew him to be a nasty bully, and she shuddered to think what would happen to Charlie if he attacked her. Olga had heard some strong accusations against him, but had never concerned herself about it.

It was a well known fact among some of the street people that Olga carried a concealed knife, and was no one to fool with, especially considering her demented mind, and her rough appearance. And so she didn't fear anyone. Olga followed carefully behind the man, staying back just far enough so that he wouldn't detect her presence. He had started walking much faster, and so had Olga, who was sure that they must be getting much closer to Charlie. Also it was quickly getting much darker out. Olga knew the area very well, and knew how and where she could get ahead of him before he caught up with Charlie. So she deviated from the alley, and came up at the edge of the alley near where Charlie was just approaching, with the man almost up to Charlie. Sensing his closeness Charlie had started to run, but in an instant he was grabbing her, and she heard a nasty laugh. However his triumph didn't last long, as Olga's knife blade plunged into his back between his ribs. He gave a sharp yelp, and then he was falling, and Charlie was up running. Olga removed the knife from the man's back, wiped it quickly on some shrubbery and put it away. Then she hurried after Charlie as fast as she could. Olga felt much shaken by the incident as she hurried home, but she felt that there was no way anyone could connect her to it. Olga had never killed anyone before, although she had found it necessary to defend herself on a few occasions. Olga hadn't eaten all day, but she didn't feel very hungry, and both she and Charlie were too upset to feel like eating anymore than a piece of bread, before they tiredly went to bed.

The next morning following their paper routes, Olga was to go to the orphanage to clean the bedrooms while the children were out of them. She was to do the rest of the building at night when the children and staff were in bed. Olga and Charlie were given a very brief orientation to the cleaning supplies and the procedures. After they cleaned the bedrooms, they went home to sleep. Olga was going to have a busy day as she was keeping her late afternoon paper route, and then going with Charlie to do the night cleaning at the orphanage. When Olga came home in the evening she had to find some food on her way home. Needless to say she was not in a very pleasant mood. Charlie hated it when Olga was nasty, so she stayed out of her way as much as possible. Olga had seen the headlines in the newspaper about the man who had been found dead in an alley. The article went on to say that he had been stabbed to death. The police couldn't understand why he had been there, so far from his place of residence. Especially considering that he was a respected business man. It was thought to be a possibility that some one had lured him there. But they did not know why.

His wallet and money were still in his pocket, and he was still wearing his wrist watch. The police were asking for the public's help, if they had any information they should come forward.

Olga and Charlie finished their cleaning at three a.m. and walked the mile home as fast as they could. Olga was going to be tired in the morning, when she got up to deliver her papers. She was hoping that everything went well for Charlie with the cleaning. Then Olga would only have the paper routes to do. She was starting to feel her age.

CHAPTER TWO

The next night went much faster, and Charlie felt that she could do the job by herself. Charlie liked the job much better than the paper routes. The following night Charlie did the work by herself and so it took her a bit longer, but Charlie didn't mind. She was so glad not to have to go out in the wet and cold and have to walk for miles in it. The following morning she did the bedrooms by herself, and then went home to sleep again. Before going to bed she carried some extra water home and took a bath. She also changed into some clean boy's clothes before going to lie down. Her shoes were in pretty bad shape. She would have to ask Olga to find her some new ones, perhaps she could find some at the thrift shop.

Olga had been given a door key to the orphanage, so that she could let herself in and out when doing the cleaning. Charlie was beginning to realize that maybe other people had better living conditions than she and Olga did. Working in a clean place with better furniture started her into doing a lot of thinking.

One morning as she was finishing the hall floor, she thought that she heard crying coming from one of the bedrooms. Then a girl about half her size got up and went to the bathroom. Charlie made a point of not looking at her. But she wondered why she was crying and sniffing as she walked to the bathroom and back. Perhaps she was lonely for a mother, Charlie thought. Charlie finished her cleaning and went home. She kept thinking about how sad the girl seemed to be. Of course there was no way that Charlie would even consider conversing with anyone.

And so Charlie's routine stayed the same, with the occasional episodes of a girl crying. Charlie chose to mind her own business.

Olga had stopped at a thrift shop on her way home from her paper route. She got Charlie some slightly used shoes and some other pants and shirts, also a jacket, so that she wouldn't look like a rag bag.

Charlie took regular baths, and was beginning to feel better about life, even though she had to work hard. Charlie was glad that winter was coming, which meant that she wouldn't have to pull weeds in the hot sun. Her hair was starting to grow a bit long and she wondered what it would be like to have long hair. Her wonderings were cut short by Olga deciding that it was time for Charlie to have a hair cut. Olga reminded her that it was safer to be a boy than do be a girl with mean old men after her. Charlie had to agree. And so she kept on playing the part with her head down and not speaking to anyone.

One night when Charlie was at the orphanage, and going to unlock the door, a man appeared suddenly in front of the door. Charlie had jumped back into the shadow just in time before the man saw her. The man proceeded to unlock the door and go in. Charlie waited a few minutes and then she unlocked the door and went in. She didn't see anyone around, so she got her equipment and went to work. As she was doing the hall again she heard the girl crying, and she thought that she heard a man's voice speaking in a whisper and low tones. She thought that she must be imagining things. Why would there be a man's voice in the bedroom? Soon the girl appeared again on her way to the bathroom and she was sniffling. Charlie was tempted to go to the bedroom and see who was there, and see what they were doing there. But she was too scared and figured that she better mind her own business. It saddened her to see the little girl so unhappy. The next night Charlie again heard the little girl crying and the sound of the man's voice. Charlie couldn't contain her curiosity any longer, so she pulled her cap down almost over her eyes, took her mop and slowly sauntered over to the bedroom. Charlie peaked in the door, and pretended to mop up a spot in front of the door. The girl was in bed hugging a teddy bear, and an old grey haired man sat in a chair. He had a book in his hand and was quietly reading to her. The man looked up from the book, and said, "My granddaughter misses her mother so much, that I am reading to her." Charlie bobbed her head up and down and left the room. Her questions had been answered.

Charlie did the janitor work, and Olga did her paper routes without any marked occurrences until just before Christmas. Then Olga told Charlie that she had saved enough money for them to rent a small house. It would take awhile to get more furniture and it would cost them money for electricity and water. But Olga felt that they could manage if they were very careful not to spend money on any thing else. Olga even squeezed out enough money for a few groceries for Christmas. Olga had eased up on Charlie since they saw less of each other. Charlie got a ten cent an hour raise in pay and a ten dollar Christmas bonus. She was never late and did a good job at whatever she was directed to do.

The weather was very cold, and it was miserably cold in the old building where they lived. It was impossible to find enough wood to heat the area other than right around the stove. Olga had a cold, and said that she just couldn't keep on working and freezing. She was going to see about a house the following day. Olga soon found out that it wasn't easy to find something that she could afford. Also people weren't anxious to rent to a crazy woman. How dependable would she be? She finally found a place that was on the edge of town on an acreage where the owner lived in a big house. He had used the small house for his hired help, and wasn't in need of it for at least a few months. It was on the same side of town as the orphanage, and so it meant that Charlie didn't have to walk any farther to work. Olga and Charlie moved into the house as soon as they could, to get out of the cold. In another six weeks the winter would be over, but for now it was extremely cold. They didn't have much furniture. Olga managed to find a few boxes and kept watch for any thing someone might throw out. Now that they had some lights, Charlie started doing more reading. She was getting an appreciation of how many different things took place in the world, and in the town around her. When the weather started to warm up, Charlie was given some extra work to do. It was necessary for her to converse with the person she had to work with. That person was the son of the manager of the orphanage. His name was Ted. He was very polite and considerate to work with. He seemed to have an appreciation of Charlie's shy manner, and tried to put her at ease. He avoided asking the questions that he was burning to ask. Of course he thought that Charlie was a boy. The orphanage had its own gardens, and a couple long green houses. Ted's father looked after the gardening. Ted explained this to Charlie and said that they were starting the seeds in the greenhouse, and in a few weeks they would have to work with the new plants. Ted said that they would have to hire a helper when the plants got bigger. He asked Charlie if she would like the job. Ted considered Charlie to be a good worker; however Charlie was too shy to give him an answer. Charlie kept thinking about it, but she didn't tell Olga about the offer, as she was sure that Olga wouldn't want her interacting that closely with anyone. Ted didn't mention the job again for a week. But one morning he asked Charlie to come with him, and he took Charlie to the greenhouse, where they had started working with the new seedlings which had to be transplanted. Ted explained the setup to Charlie and asked her to help him. Charlie was afraid to say no, and so she did what she was asked. Charlie found the work was easy and interesting. She looked forward to coming again the next day. Life started to take on a new meaning for Charlie after she entered the world of plants. It was something that she had never given a second thought to. Now she looked forward to going to work, and could hardly wait to get her cleaning finished each morning so that she could go to the greenhouses. Olga noticed that Charlie had brightened up and seemed more alive. Olga wondered what had brought about the change in Charlie, and started questioning her about what was going on at work. Charlie was also earning more money as she was putting in more hours. Charlie told her that she was helping with the plants for the gardens, but she was careful not to mention Ted's name.

A couple of days later Olga didn't get up early to deliver papers. Charlie wondered what was going on, but she was afraid to approach Olga about it. Later on in the day Olga got up and Charlie could see that she looked and acted sick. She was very pale and shaky and she seemed to have a cough. Olga managed to get ready and left to do her evening route. When she returned, she had some scavenged food, but she went right to bed without eating. Charlie was very concerned, but she couldn't stay home with her, as she had to go to work.

The following morning when Charlie went to bed she heard Olga doing a lot of coughing. Olga got up late again. She told Charlie that she had given up her morning paper route, as she was too tired to get out in the cold so early in the morning. Olga had bought some cough medicine, but it didn't help much. However she insisted that she had to do her evening route. This time when she came home she didn't have any food, and she looked even sicker than when she had left. Charlie knew that if she wanted to eat she would have to buy some food. She was afraid to talk to strangers. She also didn't have any money, as Olga always handled the money, and hid it away in different hiding places. Charlie had never paid much attention to where Olga hid the money, as she had never considered spending any. So she had to do some thinking and searching, until she finally found some. All the time she was being careful not to disturb Olga. Olga sat up and grumbled once and then went back to sleep. So Charlie printed out a short grocery list to take to the store.

She hadn't been in a store since she was too small to leave home alone. She was afraid to buy very many things as she wasn't very knowledgeable about the cost of food. She also wasn't much of a cook, never having had much food to cook. So she printed bread, eggs, milk, wieners, and oatmeal, and with shaky knees presented it to the clerk in the store. The girl behind the counter was very nice and helped Charlie count out the right amount of money. Charlie left the store feeling very good about her accomplishment. This was a new experience for her, and she had accomplished it without anything bad occurring. Maybe other people weren't as bad as Olga insisted that they were. Besides, Charlie was realizing more and more that she had to do things, and think things out for herself instead of letting Olga dictate to her about her every move. So Charlie decided that it was time for her to show a little independence, and she managed to make supper for herself and Olga. Olga didn't eat much as she was still feeling under the weather. But she didn't complain about anything either.

That night when Charlie went to work, there was a new bounce to her step. That is, until she was nearly at the orphanage, and she knew that someone was coming behind her. At first she thought that it was just someone headed in the same direction as she was going. But then when she turned around and stopped, the person behind her stopped also. Charlie tried this three times, and then became convinced that someone was indeed following her. She didn't have Olga to help her out this time. So she stopped behind a big tree and waited, hoping that whoever it was would pass by her. She waited, standing very still, hardly daring to breathe. Soon she heard footsteps, and then a form appeared. It passed her for a very short distance and then stopped and turned around. Charlie hurriedly hid behind the tree. The person stood very still for about a minute. Charlie's heart was pounding so hard that she was sure that whoever it was would be able to hear it. The person came back a few steps and stopped again, peering around in the darkness. Charlie held her breath, waiting, while a dreadful feeling of fear overcame her. She didn't have any weapon to defend herself with, if someone should attack her. Her pulse was pounding in her head and her hands were cold and clammy with tension. The person had moved a couple of steps closer to Charlie's tree.

Charlie was frozen with fear. She couldn't move if she wanted to. Then Charlie heard the person speak out loud; "Where the hell did that boy go? I was just going to smack him around a little bit, just have a little bit of fun with him? He doesn't look like he could fight his way out of a wet paper bag. Yep, he sure gave me the slip. But there'll be another time."

Just then a car light appeared. The car stopped, and Charlie quickly took a peek around the tree. It was a policeman getting out of the car and heading towards the person stalking her. The policeman called out to the man to stay where he was, as he wanted to talk to him. Charlie breathed a big sigh of relief. The police put handcuffs on the man and directed him to get into the car. Charlie waited until the car drove away. Then she ran for the orphanage as fast as her legs could go. She was only a few minutes late. Her ordeal had not lasted as long as it had seemed to her. But she was quite shaken up from her experience, and it took her awhile to settle down. The following morning, she was glad when Ted came around to accompany her to the greenhouse. She felt like telling him about it, but didn't know if she should, so she kept quiet about it. Ted noticed that she seemed rather agitated about something. But when he asked her if there was anything wrong, she said that she was just tired. So Ted left it at that.

When Charlie got home from work, she made some breakfast and went to bed. She didn't go to sleep right away as she kept thinking about what she could do to protect herself. She decided to talk to Olga about it, and fell asleep with that thought in mind.

When Charlie awoke, she discovered that Olga had already left. So Charlie decided to do something that she had never done before. She went up town to walk around and look in store windows. Charlie was amazed at how many things were in the stores. She read several of the advertisements for different products, also about up coming events. One advertisement particularly caught her eye. It asked the question, "Would you like to be able to defend yourself? Even against people who are larger and stronger than you are?" Charlie thought to herself, that is exactly what I would like to be able to do. The advertisement said that there would be five classes, one each week in the evening on Thursdays. The best and most important factor to Charlie was that it was free. But could she muster up the courage to go? That was the issue that kept rolling around in her mind all the way home. She knew that she would have to keep it a secret from Olga if she did decide to go.

That night when she went to work she carried an old stove poker. It was a hefty chunk of iron and was a good length for swinging at someone's head, if need be.

All during her shift Charlie kept thinking about all the things she had seen in the store windows, especially the ladies clothes. Charlie was starting to develop a slightly rounder and softer figure in certain areas. She wondered what she would look like in the girl's clothes. But then she couldn't think of any reason why she or anyone else would want to wear them. They would be useless for doing most jobs. Some things looked like they would be pretty cold in the winter. Charlie was glad to get clothes that kept her warm.

The next day Charlie decided that it was time for her to try talking to Olga about life in general. She told Olga about the man who had followed her and about how she carried a poker to work for protection. She told Olga that she is no longer a child and how her thinking and circumstances in life are changing. She tried to impress on Olga just how much more aware she has become of the world around her. How she needed to have some spending money, and learn how to manage money.

Olga told Charlie that she had talked enough for one day, and would talk about it later. Charlie had expected that dealing with Olga wouldn't be easy and wondered just how she could get her to really discuss the matter. Olga was good at avoiding complicated issues.

CHAPTER THREE

When Charlie went to work the next night she was still thinking about some of the changes that she would like in her life. In the morning when Ted came to get her to go to the greenhouse, she was still mulling things over in her mind.

Ted told her to sit down for a few minutes, as he had something to discuss with her. He went on to tell her that they had hired an extra cleaning person for the Orphanage. This would mean that she wouldn't have to do as much cleaning. Then he told her that she could have a full time job working in the Greenhouse if she wanted it. Charlie was very surprised, and at first she didn't know what to say. Finally she told Ted that she would think about it and let him know in a couple days. Now she had something else to think about. She would love to work full time in the greenhouse, but it meant that someone else would have to be found to replace her in the janitor job. When Charlie got home from work she heard Olga coughing again. Charlie thought about what a cold miserable job Olga has delivering papers in all kinds of weather. She knew that Olga needed an inside job. It suddenly came to Charlie's realization that Olga could take over her janitor job. She would only have to work the night shift, now that they had hired another person. And it would mean that Charlie would be free to work full time with the plants.

Charlie was very tired, so she decided to talk to Olga about it later on in the evening. She hoped that Olga wouldn't be in a disagreeable mood.

At supper time Charlie told Olga about the offer she got to work full time in the greenhouse. She asked Olga if she would do the janitor work instead of delivering papers. Olga said that she would think about it, and that she would have to give the "newspaper" notice that she was quitting.

This gave Charlie a small hope that Olga would give up her paper route. Charlie didn't like the waiting for answers as she was anxious for the greenhouse job. She had also been thinking about getting her own pay cheque. Olga got the cheque for the janitor work. This meant that Charlie didn't have any money other than what Olga gave her which was very minimal. Charlie was growing up, and it was time for Olga to realize it. She couldn't keep treating Charlie like an ignorant child. Many thoughts were going through Charlie's mind lately. She wanted to be a girl! She hated the cap that Olga insisted that she wear. She hated the bulky boy's pants that made her look like a slouchy boy. But most of all she hated trying to convince people that she was a boy who had speech problems.

The next three days were agonizing for Charlie, as she waited for Olga to make her decision about the job. However her agony quickly turned into jubilation, when Olga agreed to take over the janitor work.

Charlie could hardly wait to tell Ted about the job changes. In the back of her mind was the intention to ask Ted, to give her, her own pay cheque. When Charlie went to work the next day, she was surprised to see another girl working in the greenhouse. She appeared to be a few years older than Charlie. Ted introduced her as Betty. He went on to explain that Betty had worked there for two years previously. Charlie felt very insecure meeting Betty, as she had never had any real contact with another girl. By the time the shift was over, Charlie had decided that Betty was a very likeable and kind person. The event of meeting another girl served to make Charlie even more determined to dress and live as a girl. She felt that if she communicated with Betty very much, Betty would soon question whether Charlie was really a boy. When Charlie asked Ted if she could get her pay cheque put in her own name, he explained to her, that she would have to have a social insurance number. He said that he would get Betty to talk to her about it, and to help her with anything else that she needed help with. The next day, Betty said that she would help her to apply for a social insurance card. She told Charlie that she should get a bank account so that she could cash her cheques. Charlie told her how much she appreciated the help. And that she had never had any social life, and was therefore ignorant of many everyday things. Charlie longed to confide in Betty about how she wanted to start living as a girl. She wanted to be able to carry on normal conversations with people.

At the end of a week, Betty suggested that they spend the morning going up town and taking care of Charlie's business. Betty took Charlie to the bank and showed her how to set up an account and how to do her general banking. She asked Charlie if she would mind if she went into a store and looked at some clothes. Charlie was glad to be able to look at clothes with someone who probably was knowledgeable about them. Charlie said, "I've never been in a clothing store before, just the Thrift Shop. So I would like to see what people are wearing." However the sales clerk kept giving Charlie disapproving looks, and kept watching her out of the corner of her eye. This made Charlie very uncomfortable. So Charlie told Betty that she would wait outside. Betty had noticed the clerk's unfriendly glances, and told Charlie to stay and to ignore her. So Charlie stayed close to Betty, who gabbled on about what she liked or disliked about the clothes she looked at. Charlie found her observations interesting and informative. They did the same thing in a couple more stores, and then Betty told Charlie that she would like to buy her lunch. They went to a Chinese restaurant and Betty ordered food that Charlie had never tasted before. Charlie was so overwhelmed by Betty's kindness that she decided to tell her the truth about herself. Charlie looked down at the table and said, "Betty, you are so kind. I have to tell you something. I can't keep pretending any more. I'm not really a boy! My mother makes me dress this way.

She thinks that it protects me from bad people. But I want to live like a normal girl." Betty looked at Charlie; she had a rather surprised look on her face. After a brief silence she said, "Charlie, I did sort of wonder about your voice, but didn't give it much thought. It is still quite a surprise to hear you say that you are not a boy. Well, if you want to be a girl, we've got a bit of work to do. But, it will be fun! It will especially be fun seeing the looks on some people's faces." Betty paused and smilingly asked, "When do you want to start?" Charlie said, "I have to wait until I have some money to buy some girl's clothes." Betty said, "Why don't you ask Ted to cash a cheque for you for your last week's pay?" "Then we can go shopping and you can get a girl's hair cut, and then you can throw that ugly cap in the garbage." Charlie had to smile. She said, "Thanks again Betty, I am so lucky that I met you. You are saving my life. It's going to be hard to wait until we can get started."

Charlie knew that she had to tell Ted that she was not a boy. She just couldn't find the right time and get up enough courage. But by the end of the week she knew that she had to tell him. She waited until near the end of her shift, and then asked to speak to him. It didn't help matters when he hesitated out of surprise, as Charlie always went around without speaking. Ted asked her to come to his small office, and invited her to sit down. Needless to say Charlie was very nervous. Betty was the only person that she had carried on a conversation with. All week Charlie was thinking about how to bring up the subject to Ted. When she went to his office, she sat with her hands squeezed together and said, Next week I'm going to look different, I'm going to surprise you. Betty is going to help me. Ted became very curious, but didn't think that he should question her about a surprise. So he smiled and said "I'll be waiting for the surprise. Don't you disappoint me now, after making me wait to see what it is". Charlie left feeling relieved that she had taken the first step in her change over to living as a girl. She even felt brave enough to ask Ted to advance her some money from her next pay cheque. Now she still had Olga to contend with. She decided to wait until after the make over, as seeing Charlie as a girl might serve to influence Olga into accepting her the way she should.

Betty and Charlie met on the morning of their day off. Charlie wasn't sure just what was in store for her. Betty said, "Leave everything to me. I have made a couple of appointments for us. Betty paused for a moment, and then she said that she thought that the trip to the beauty parlor for a haircut should come first. So they went to the beauty salon where Betty had made the appointment. Nobody had ever seen Charlie's hair, as she wore a big man's cap that she kept pulled down low. When she took off the cap a lot of straggly curly hair was exposed to the world for the first time. Betty asked the beautician to cut Charlie's hair into a nicely shaped style that would suit her face and would make her look feminine. So after a shampoo and the first conditioner that Charlie had ever experienced, she got a shapely hair cut. When Charlie looked in the mirror she could hardly believe that it was her. Betty was very pleased at the transformation that had taken place. She took the cap and threw it in the garbage, as she said, "Good riddance! They then went to a store to buy Charlie some lady's slacks. Charlie felt ten pounds lighter when she got rid of the bulky men's pants. They also bought Charlie two tops for work. That pretty well used up all of Charlie's money. Since they were in such a good mood, they went for lunch. Then Charlie had to go home and face Olga. Charlie decided to buy something for supper, to put her mother in a better mood. The last few months they were able to buy groceries, rather than eating the leftovers from the restaurants. Charlie couldn't see herself eating that way ever again

When Olga got up from her nap, Charlie had supper ready. Olga had to look twice at Charlie before she realized that Charlie looked different. Then she asked, "What is going on? Why did you get a fancy haircut? It is time that I gave you a haircut." To which Charlie said, "Oh no, I'm never wearing that cap again; from now on I'm living like the girl that I am. Olga started getting red in the face and looking mad. She warned Charlie not to talk back to her or she would lay a licking on her. Her threat did not carry much weight with Charlie, as Charlie had grown taller and done some filling out in the last year, plus she had her mind made up, that no matter what happened, she was staying a girl. So Charlie told Olga exactly what she felt about things. Olga continued to grumble, but seemed to be accepting the fact that Charlie was not going to be intimidated. Charlie had reached her sixteenth birthday two weeks prior. Of course she did not think it was anything special, as it never had been in the past. Celebrations had never been part of Charlie's childhood.

When Charlie went to work the next day, Betty was already at the greenhouse. She smiled at Charlie and told her that she was anxious to see what Ted was going to say, and to see the surprised look on his face. When Ted came in, he glanced over at the girls who had their backs towards him. They were busy working with the plants, and he went about his business. Then he stopped and turned around. Why were there two girls? And where was Charlie? Ted walked over to where the girls were.

Ted said, "Betty, do you know where Charlie is? Who is your friend? I don't think that we have met."

The girls turned around, and Betty said, "Good morning Ted, I would like you to meet my friend, and your friend; Charlie."

At first Ted stared at Charlie with a very puzzled expression on his face. Then a surprised and questioning look appeared on his face. He suddenly recalled that Charlie had told him that she was going to have a surprise for him. Ted still had a look of disbelief on his face, but he suddenly burst out laughing. Then Betty and Charlie started to laugh at the different expressions that crossed Ted's face. Ted said, "Is that really you Charlie? This is quite a surprising and difficult thing, to realize that you are really a girl. You do make a terrific looking girl; I mean you are a terrific looking girl, much too pretty to be a boy."

Charlie turned red and squirmed with discomfort, as she was not used to carrying on such a personal conversation, especially with someone of the opposite sex.

Charlie managed to say, "Thank you! Ted, but we had better get back to work or you won't be very pleased with us."

And so the girls went back to work, chattering away like a pair of happy magpies. Charlie felt like she was on top of the world. And Betty felt and looked as pleased as the cat that drank the cream.

THE PAPER GIRL

CHAPTER FOUR

The atmosphere of the greenhouse had taken on a sunny disposition, both inside and outside, as the days became brighter and warmer. And the young people felt more and more lighthearted, as the days of spring soon became the days of summer. Now the work shifted to more outside work. The sun was hot enough to require the wearing of a straw hat. And the gardening staff was acquiring golden sun tans.

One day Charlie got a big surprise, when at lunch time, Ted brought a young man over to meet her and Betty. Ted introduced him as his cousin; Dave Turner. He went on to explain that Dave wanted to visit Ted's family for awhile. Dave was trying to decide what to do with his future, now that he had recently graduated from university.

From then on Dave showed up every day to visit with Charlie and Betty, and the rest of the staff. Charlie noticed that Dave spent most of his time talking with her and a girl named Jean.

Since Dave was very good looking, and had a witty, charming way about him. Charlie felt drawn to him.

Charlie was too inexperienced to realize that Dave was a smooth talker, and that he was flirting with her.

Betty could see that Dave was making a big impression on Charlie. However Betty was afraid that if she said anything about it, Charlie would think that she was jealous. And so Betty did not say anything to Charlie about it. Instead she approached Ted about the feeling she had that Dave was "smooth talking" Charlie. She reminded him that Charlie was totally inexperienced, and hence, very naïve. Charlie could easily be misled by Dave's sweet talk. She asked Ted if he could some how diplomatically warn Charlie.

Ted was well educated concerning his Cousin Dave's selfish ways. He knew about some of Dave's past activities, that Ted personally disapproved of. He would have to think this over very carefully. It was a touchy situation and he thought a lot of Charlie, he certainly didn't want her to get hurt. Dealing with Dave was a challenge he wished that he did not have to be involved in. Ted assured Betty that he would do something, but it might not be something that could be resolved over night. Betty went away, relieved that at least Ted was aware, and working on the situation.

Several days later Ted noticed that Dave was hanging around Charlie when she was trying to work. So Ted waited for an opportunity to inform Dave that he was interfering with Charlie's efforts to get her work done. Ted told Dave that he was spending too much time in the greenhouse. That he should spend some time in town or go for a drive somewhere to put some variety in his holiday. He went on to remind Dave that he had previously been in trouble because of making bad decisions. Dave didn't take too kindly to Ted telling him what he should do. It was not in Dave's personality to accept any kind of correction from another person, especially his cousin.

Dave didn't come around for a couple days. But, then he showed up about three days later. He approached Charlie at the end of the day, and invited her to go for a drive with him. Charlie had never ridden in a car and so at first she was speechless. Ted was not present at the time that the invitation was extended. So it was easy for Dave to convince Charlie that she should go with him. At first Charlie was quite overwhelmed at the feeling of moving so fast, and at seeing so many new things. She thought that it was quite a wonderful experience. Dave insisted that she sit close to him. This prompted Charlie to think that she was having a glorious time. She got a warming pleasant feeling when she sat close to Dave. When he took her home, he played the gentleman to the hilt, opening the car door for her and walking her to her door. Then he took her hand and squeezed it, while telling her what a wonderful time he had sharing her company. Charlie felt tingly all over, and her knees went weak like maybe they wouldn't hold her and she feared that she might collapse. Charlie's pulse was racing, and she was afraid that Dave could hear it pounding away in her chest. Dave went on to tell her what a beautiful and smart girl she was. Charlie realized that she had not contributed much to their conversation, but she loved the way Dave complimented her. So when he asked her if she would go again the next afternoon, she did not hesitate before saying yes.

That night Charlie dreamed about Dave. It was all she could think about the next day, as she moved through life like she was floating on a rosy cloud.

Betty observed her out of the corner of her eye. She had a sinking feeling that Charlie was infatuated with Dave. Her guess was that Dave was working his self centered magic on her. He seemed to be a very smooth operator. It greatly disturbed Betty to have to stand by and watch Charlie get hurt by this ruthless Romeo. However for now she would have to stand by, be patient and see what transpired between Dave and Charlie. Dave took Charlie for a drive almost every day for two weeks. Finally Betty asked Charlie why she was always busy after work. She told Charlie that she would like to share a day of shopping with her. Betty hoped that she would be able to find out what was going on. Charlie was undecided about what she should do. She wanted to talk to Betty, about the scary wonderful feelings she had when she was with Dave, but on the other hand she was afraid to mention it, even to Betty. She finally agreed to go shopping with Betty, as Betty was very persistent about it.

The girls spent the day shopping for what they considered as being necessary items. They ended the day with dinner and conversation. Dave soon became the main topic. Betty was dismayed to realize how involved the situation had become for Charlie. She doubted that Dave was very emotionally involved. Now she had something to really worry about. She tried to explain to Charlie, that she understood what she was experiencing, and that she should try not to be so dependant on Dave's companionship. Of course her logic was falling on deaf ears. Charlie was just too infatuated to care what Betty thought. In the next few weeks, Dave convinced Charlie that he loved her, and that he wanted her to spend the weekends with him. He had taken on a part time job and got a place of his own. Of course Charlie was as happy as a lark, at the prospect of being so intimately involved with Dave. However, Charlie was able to keep Dave at bay, when he pressured her to have a sexual relationship with him. She was afraid to get that involved, after what Betty had told her. She had to fight her natural urges and her temptations. They spent several weekends together. Dave always had to have some wine. Charlie was afraid to drink any. Also she noticed that Dave became very bossy after drinking it. But she was too blindly in love, to pay attention to any negative thoughts she might have. She disregarded Dave's occasional push or slight arm twisting as being justified, because she moved too slowly. She did not comprehend that Dave was in charge of everything, including her. One night when he had drunk more than usual, he ordered her to get something for him. When she did not jump right up to do it, he gave her a stinging slap on the behind. Charlie jumped up in surprise yelling, "Ouch that hurt! What's the matter with you?" Dave laughed and then his face turned ugly as he yelled at Charlie, "Don't talk back to me, don't ever talk back to me!" Charlie became frightened when she saw his face, and heard the anger in his voice. So she asked Dave if he would take her home. Of course this only served to make him even more angry and violent. In a flash his fist lashed out and caught her on the side of the head. Charlie felt a sharp pain shoot through her head, and her world turned black. When she came to, she was being held by Dave who was sitting on the floor with her. He was busy telling her how sorry he was. Charlie was rather dizzy at first, but after a few minutes her head cleared. Other than having a headache, she felt fine. Dave was putting on a very convincing performance, about how remorseful he was, and how much he loved and needed her. Without hesitation Charlie accepted everything he said.

The next week end Betty asked Charlie to go out with her and her boyfriend. They were planning to go to a dance. Of course Charlie was not enthusiastic about going, because she did not want to go with any one but Dave, plus she did not know how to dance. But Betty assured her that she would teach her enough to get by with.

She told her how much fun it was to whirl around the floor in time to the music. Betty was so convincing that Charlie agreed to go. Charlie was also not looking forward to another tense weekend with Dave.

When Betty and her friend Arnold came to pick Charlie up for the dance, there was another man with them. Betty introduced him as "Gordon," a friend of Arnold's. Charlie observed that Gordon was very good looking. He had a very polite manner and way of speaking. As the evening passed, Charlie came to realize what a happy relaxed time she was having. There were no demands made, and everyone did a lot of laughing, as Gordon knew and told a lot of jokes. He had a very funny way about telling them. This was a really new experience for Charlie.

As the next week seemed to fly by for Charlie, in the back of her mind was a nagging worry that Dave would show up. She could not help feeling guilty for enjoying herself so much, when she knew that Dave would not like the way she went with someone else. At the end of the week Dave did show up, and insisted that she take a ride with him. Dave drove to the park and stopped the car in the parking area. He was unusually pleasant, as he managed to get as much information as he could about Charlie's date with Betty. Then Dave was very quiet for a brief time. All of a sudden he got a harsh tone to his voice, and started bombarding Charlie, with nasty accusations about her behavior. His face appeared to have a hateful expression, and Charlie braced herself for what might follow this cruel and bitter outburst. She was not to be disappointed, as Dave grabbed her arm and gave it a painful, pinching twist. Then he reached over and smacked her on the side of her face. This brought tears to her eyes. Dave jeered at her for being a crybaby, and told her what an unfaithful Judas she was. Charlie was afraid to stay in the car with him, so she opened the door and jumped out. Dave yelled at her, "Where do you think that you are going?" Charlie did not hesitate and took off running as fast as she could. Of course Dave ran after her, all the while yelling threats about what was going to happen to her when he caught her. Charlie was in very good shape for running, as she worked outside most of the day, and had to walk everywhere. So after a brief time Dave realized that he could not catch her. Angrily he gave up chasing her and returned to the car. He drove around with the car hoping to catch her at the other end of the park. But Charlie anticipated his idea, and had taken a detour. She watched until she saw his car pass, and then ran down a side street that bordered the park. It did not take

Charlie long to get home, as she was fearful of Dave finding her. Charlie did not move very far from home the following day, as she did not want to risk meeting up with Dave.

Charlie had to go to work on Monday, but she did not think that Dave would get up early enough to catch her. Charlie was so upset about the whole episode, that on their lunch break, she told Betty about what had ensued between her and Dave. Of course Betty was outraged, and wanted to tell Ted about it. But Charlie begged her not to. She did not want to stir up any problems between Ted and his cousin. Although she did not know how she was going to deal with the situation. She would just have to take one thing at a time. Charlie had considering questions in her mind.

Maybe Dave would give up on the idea of ever seeing her again. Would she really want that? After all she had special feelings for him, he needed her. How could she let him down? He had told her how bad his life was, did she want him to hurt? She wanted to help him, but she was now afraid of his anger. Why had she made him so angry? What was the matter with her? Why should she go out and have a good time, when Dave needed her? All these thoughts and doubts whirled around in her head. Then all of a sudden a light bulb came on in her head. What about me? I feel awful about my relationship with Dave. If I love Dave why are things so bad? Why is it wrong for me to go out with people, who are pleasant and fun to be with? I have to make a choice or else go crazy. I don't want to be hit by Dave ever again. I feel like I'm bound up in misery. The only solution is to stay away from Dave. I hope that he can find someone else to care for him. But I can't handle his life, it is too complicated. That's it; I won't go with Dave again. Besides I am afraid of what he might do next.

That weekend, Arnold and Gordon came to town and Betty asked Charlie to go to the dance again, as Gordon had enjoyed Charlie's company so very much the last time that they had gone out together. Charlie was only too happy to take advantage of another opportunity to spend a fun evening with her friends.

During the evening the conversation included some serious talk at times. Gordon told Charlie about his job as a railway locomotive engineer. Charlie was fascinated. But she felt very inferior, when Gordon asked her what she planned to do with her life. Charlie had not given much thought to the puzzle of her future. When Charlie said that she had no idea, Gordon explained to her about how much information she could get by going to the library.

Betty volunteered to go with her. Charlie had not realized that there was such a place. She read every newspaper that she could, but had never read a book.

When Charlie first went to the library, she looked around in amazement at all the shelves of books. She asked the Librarian hundreds of questions. She found out about some adult education courses. The Librarian suggested that she start by taking home a couple books to read, before she got involved in any thing further.

Charlie agreed with her and chose two books that the Librarian recommended. One was fiction and the other was of a more serious nature.

After three days Charlie was back at the library to get some more books. Charlie had entered a new world, a wonderful world where she could find out about anything and everything that she wanted. She was like a sponge soaking up everything in her path. Betty was amused by her enthusiasm, but disappointed that she spent almost every free moment reading. Charlie even read an informative book about trains and railways. She thought that Gordon was an important addition to her existence. He was the special one who turned her on to this wonderful new way of life. So she wanted to have at least a small amount of knowledge, about what went on in his world. He was the person responsible for getting her involved in seeking out information, concerning some kind of career. She certainly could not disappoint him, after he showed so much faith in her. After all he was the one who had opened the door to so many new and interesting things.

The next time that Charlie went to the library, the Librarian told her about some adult education classes that would soon be available at the high school. The classes were held in the evening and would not interfere with her work. She explained to Charlie what the subjects were, and how to go about registering for them.

When Charlie told Betty about her plans, Betty was almost as excited as Charlie was. Betty liked Charlie immensely and wanted her to have a chance to make something of her life. It also made Betty stop and ask herself what she, herself planned to do with her life. Betty had completed grade twelve, but had not thought too seriously about what she would do later on in life. She was happy to go to work and earn some money after she graduated. But now she was beginning to consider that maybe she might want more out of life than working in a greenhouse. She enjoyed working with plants, but there did not seem to be much future in it.

So it was Betty who spent time questioning the Librarian, about places where she might take further education or training. The Librarian had lists of colleges and trade schools. Betty decided that at the end of the week, she would get together with Charlie and talk about their future.

One evening when Charlie was coming home from some last minute grocery shopping, she thought that someone was following her. It was late evening and Charlie was taking her time, just enjoying the fresh air and day dreaming. It suddenly occurred to her that someone was steadily taking the same turns that she was, and pausing when ever she did. For no known reason she got a feeling of dread, like a premonition that something bad was about to happen. Her mind immediately flashed back to her last encounter with Dave, and she wondered why he had not contacted her again. She was sure that he had been too angry, just to let things go. The feeling of uneasiness took hold of her, and she dodged behind a building, and into a dark doorway, to see if anyone would appear along the street from where she had come. She waited for at least ten minutes, before she heard quiet footsteps coming along on the sidewalk. Charlie waited; barely breathing, she listened and waited in dreaded anticipation of who she would see. All of a sudden the footsteps stopped. So did Charlie's breathing. It seemed like minutes went by, until Charlie was forced to take in some air as quietly as she could. Then the person started to move again. But moving slowly and making halting movements. Charlie thought it sounded like someone searching around. She shrunk back in the doorway as tight as she could, hoping, that the footsteps would continue on their way. To her surprise and relief, they did start up.

The footsteps had taken on a regular paced sound. Charlie waited until they had faded away. Then she carefully and cautiously made her way back to the sidewalk. She could see a figure moving up the street ahead of her. Charlie walked very slowly, as she stayed as close to the inside of the sidewalk as she could, until she got to the intersection. Then she turned the corner, and ran as fast as she could. She had run for two blocks, when she saw a car parked up ahead which looked a lot like Dave's car. So she crossed to the other side of the street, always looking to see if there was any sign of Dave around. Maybe it was a car similar to Dave's, and she was over reacting, she thought to herself. But never the less, she was not taking any chances. Charlie made it home in record time. She ran into the house and locked the door, then sank into a chair as her legs started to tremble. Charlie realized that the trembling was caused by the release of the tension she had been under. At first Charlie did not put the light on. She could see the street from the window in front of the house, and she could see part of the side yard. Charlie sat still in the chair until she was calmed down enough that her legs stopped trembling. She was also listening for any unusual sound outside. Charlie peeked into Olga's room to see if she had been disturbed, when Charlie came into the house and hurriedly closed the door. Charlie was assured that Olga was sleeping soundly, by the sound of her heavy breathing. Olga always slept very soundly. She was getting too old for the amount of exercise she got all day. Charlie worried about her, but she did not know what to do, as Olga was very stubborn and determined. Charlie sat listening for a few more minutes, but did not hear anything. So she took a shower and had some hot chocolate to calm her nerves, before going to bed. She could not go to sleep for awhile, as unsettling thoughts kept whirling around in her head.

CHAPTER FIVE

Charlie woke up with a start and sat bolt upright in bed. She had been dreaming that someone was chasing her down a long dark corridor. And that the corridor ended in outer space, which had no bottom. It took a few seconds of wakefulness to orientate her to her surroundings. She let out a big sigh of relief as she looked around the room. The hands on the clock indicated to her that she had better hurry, if she was going to get to work on time. Charlie did not have time to dwell on the previous evening's occurrences. She had to walk fast and sometimes run, to get to work on time. Lately she had been thinking about what a luxury it would be to own a bicycle. She also considered the drawbacks to that idea; being that she could not ride a bike, and also she did not know anything about them. Charlie was puffing when she got to work, and Ted teased her about not getting to bed early. Ted didn't seem to be rushing off as usual. So Charlie got up enough nerve to ask him if he knew anything about bicycles. Ted, having had a normal boyhood, had ridden bike for years. Ted told her some of his less fortunate experiences with a bicycle. Times that he could now laugh about. Ted went on to say that he could fix almost anything that went wrong with a bike. He even went so far as to offer any assistance she might need with a bicycle. As far as Charlie was concerned she could not ask for anything better than that. So she quickly said," Thank you Ted, I'm really going to think about this. I will talk to you about it again tomorrow." Then they both set about their work, and both had a smile on their face.

When Charlie got home from work, she looked in the newspaper for advertisements for bicycles for sale. Since she did not have much money, it was rather useless to be looking at the different prices. Charlie felt pretty discouraged and felt embarrassed to have to tell Ted that she could not afford a bicycle.

The next day she avoided having to talk to Ted, until he came and asked her about the bike. Charlie hedged around the subject of when she was, and where she was going to buy it. Ted was astute enough to suspect what was going on. So Ted said, "Charlie, I have still got my bicycle that I hardly ever ride anymore, why don't I help you to learn to ride on it? And then you can buy one later on" Charlie could hardly believe her ears. But the smile on her face was saying a big yes. Ted had to laugh at her expression. He quickly said, "After work tonight, come over to the house with me and we will take a look at it. And maybe you could try it out then."

So that is what they did. At first Charlie was afraid to get on, but with a lot of coaxing and assurances, she finally decided to get up on the seat, while Ted held the bike.

At first Charlie did a lot of tipping over. But she soon learned the proper way of steering, so that she could ride a ways. She rode until nearly dark, and then Ted asked her to come over again the next evening for more riding practice. When Charlie went to Ted's place the following evening, he came out of the garage with a wide smile on his face and said, "This is my sister's bike, she left it behind when she went to college. She apparently does not want it any more. So I am pretty sure that you could buy it on a monthly basis of a few dollars per month. That way you could have a bike right away. Charlie was so surprised that she stood with her mouth open for a couple seconds. To think that she could own a bike so easily astonished her, "Oh boy! Great!" she exclaimed, "It s a deal if you are sure about this. I am so lucky, thank you Ted! You are the best guy that I know." Ted looked really pleased, although in the back of his mind he was aware that Charlie probably did not know very many guys. Ted suggested that they go riding for while. Charlie was riding well enough that she could have ridden the bike home. But Ted was in no hurry to have her do that, as he so much enjoyed her new found happiness. There was such an air of childlike innocence about her that drew him like a magnet. Ted told her to come over the next two evenings, and they would ride together to give her practice.

Charlie had to tell Ted that she could come the next evening, but the following evening was Saturday, and she had promised Betty to go with her to the dance. There was no way Charlie could miss that. She didn't know why, but she neglected to tell Ted that she was paired off with Gordon. Perhaps it was because she liked Ted just as much as she liked Gordon. Although Gordon seemed more sophisticated in some ways, she felt more at ease with Ted. She then thought of Dave, but she did not want to spoil the moment by asking Ted about his whereabouts. So they said their good byes and each went their way.

Charlie was looking forward to the dance with great anticipation. Perhaps it was because she was anxious to tell Gordon about her registration for night classes. She knew that he would be pleased that she was taking his advice concerning her future.

Once again the couples had a very enjoyable evening. Charlie felt sad that it had to end, as they gave her a ride home. Gordon gave her a swift kiss and she ran into the house quickly, so that he wouldn't see her sad expression.

Charlie slept in the next morning, until she heard someone pounding on the door. When she opened the door, there was a policeman standing there. Charlie's knees felt weak as she listened to and digested the question the officer was asking her.

"Is Olga your mother? Is she at home?" A great feeling of dread enveloped her. Charlie hadn't checked her room last night as she usually did. She rushed to Olga's room with a panicky feeling overtaking her. She breathed in a huge sigh of relief, when she saw that Olga was in bed, sound asleep. She reported the fact to the officer. But he wouldn't be satisfied until he looked for himself. He explained that it was a routine that he had to carry out. Charlie was very curious to know why he had come to check on Olga. The officer went on to disclose that there had been a vicious murder the previous night. The victim was an elderly woman. She had been so badly beaten that it was impossible to identify her. Someone had thought that Olga still delivered papers and that she was in a vulnerable position. So she was a person that they were checking on. The officer apologized for upsetting Charlie. After the police had left, Charlie sat for awhile pondering over Olga's safety when she was out alone so much. She had to walk to and from work at odd hours. Charlie remembered some of the scares she herself had experienced. Besides Olga was always so tired and frequently had a cough. Charlie decided that Olga was getting too old to be working as a janitor. Charlie had read about older people being able to get a pension from the government when they got to be a certain age. But Charlie did not know what the age was. She decided that the next day she would go to the library and get the answers to her questions.

 Charlie realized that in spite of Olga's brusque manner, she loved Charlie enough to have always attempted to find her something to eat. She had to appreciate Olga's distrust of the rest of the world. Charlie recalled all the "dumpster" meals they had shared. It was the best that Olga could manage. And so Charlie couldn't fault her for not providing the best of childhood experiences. It was especially tough for Olga because she didn't trust anyone. She was totally self reliant. But now in her old age she was going to have to pay attention to what Charlie could do for her.

The next day at work, Charlie told Ted that she did not have much time for bike riding. Ted was curious, and asked about her date at the dance. Charlie told him about it and then went on to tell him about the murder and about her concerns for Olga. Of course Ted was able to tell her that Olga could get old age security when she reached the age of sixty five. "Well, Charlie said, she was old enough to get it last year."

Ted went on to explain that she had to apply for it at a government office, and that it could take two or three months to get a cheque. This information saved Charlie a trip to the library. Besides it was much more enjoyable to spend the time with Ted. Although he did not want to give up the times that the spent together, Ted assured her that she was ready to take the bike home. She was able to ride anywhere she pleased.

It was a happy, smiling Charlie who sped along home on her new bicycle. She was so excited that she called Olga outside to look at it. Of course Olga's first thought and questions were, "How much. And how can you pay for it?" But nothing was going to dampen Charlie's sunny outlook on life. Not even Olga's negativity.

CHAPTER SIX

Betty and Charlie had a day off, so they decided to go shopping and to have lunch together. After that they decided to go to a movie. In fact it was the first movie that Charlie had ever attended. She was very impressed by the large screen and sound. Betty bought popcorn which was also a first for Charlie. This prompted them, to afterwards, have a discussion about what a boring and do without childhood Charlie had.

"But then, Charlie said, I seemed to have survived without too many bad effects from it. Perhaps people don't really need all the things that they buy just because they have money." Betty had to agree that Charlie seemed to be quite normal. And then they had a good laugh about what was considered to be normal.

Betty gave Charlie a ride to the corner a few blocks from her place, as Charlie insisted that she could walk the rest of the way home. It was dusk and she was sure that she would be home long before dark.

After she had walked a short ways, she heard a child's voice yelling, "No, no, no."

Charlie quickened her step, and as she hurried onwards, the voice became louder and louder, with an ever increasing tone of panic. The sound was coming from a couple of old buildings near an alley. Charlie cautiously, but quickly made her way down close to the side of a building. As she crept up to the side of the building where the yelling was taking place, she took a peek around the corner of it. What she saw turned her caution to rage. A large scruffy looking man was pulling along by the arms; a small girl who appeared to be about seven or eight years old. Charlie ducked back and started looking around for some kind of weapon that she could use against the cruel brute. Luckily, she almost tripped over a chunk of two by four that was lying in the grass. Charlie did not waste any time getting it up. Then she peeked around the corner again. The man was on her side of the alley near the building. And he was walking with his back to Charlie, as he tugged and yanked and pulled the girl along. All the while he was laughing and taunting the little girl about what a nice little morsel she was, and how he was going to show her a good time. Of course the desperate sounding child continued to yell, "No" and begged him to let her go. Charlie became even more angry and repulsed. She waited until he was right at the corner. Then she jumped out and swung the two by four with all her might. Bang! Right on the top of his head! The man suddenly stopped his tirade and hit the ground with an enormous thud. He moaned and moved around, this scared Charlie into thinking that he might get up and attack her. So she proceeded to give him another good wallop on the head. There was suddenly a large amount of blood, which scared Charlie even more. She now was afraid that maybe she had killed him, and a vision of jail bars flashed through her mind. The little girl was standing as if frozen to the spot, with wide staring eyes, while trembling vigorously.

Charlie was jolted into action by the appearance of the terror which the little girl displayed. Charlie grabbed her by the hand and said, "Come on! We had better get out of here!"

The girl did not give any resistance as she hurried her along for the next few blocks, some times running, and some times walking. When Charlie got to her house, she hurried inside with the little girl.

Once they were inside, Charlie sat down on a chair to get her breath back and to try to calm her nerves. In her mind she was picturing the sight of the bleeding man and regretting having to take such strong measures. But when she looked at the poor dirty, sad looking, bad smelling child, she decided that she had no other choice. She shuddered to think what would have befallen the girl if she had not come upon them. With this realization, all guilt evaporated from Charlie's mind.

So Charlie told the girl that everything would be alright. That she was safe now, and that she would be getting a bath, which would make her feel better.

As Charlie bathed the girl, she realized how malnourished she was, she could almost count her ribs. The girl had not spoken a word as yet. So Charlie asked her what her name was. She timidly replied that her name was "Sophie." She said that her mother was very sick in the hospital, and that her dad had said that she was not coming home again. Her dad was usually gone, and when he came home he had strong smelling breath and watery eyes. He usually wobbled around and then went to bed. If she wanted food she had to find it herself.

Charlie had to shampoo her hair three times to get it clean, and Sophie had rather scaly feet and knees. Sophie went on to say that if she did not clean the house up, her dad would hit her and swear at her. Sometimes he brought a strange woman home. Sophie would stay in her room, and then go outside as soon as she woke up. She did not like any of her dad's friends. Now that she had summer holidays from school, she did not know what to do with herself. Her dad had got kicked out of the house they rented, and now they lived in a very small apartment in a dirty old building. The other people who lived there were scary and mean looking. There were lots of fighting, yelling and swearing. Sophie went on to say that she had hardly anything to eat. One time she asked a woman for some food, and the woman swore at her, and gave her a kick. Then the woman told her dad, and he scolded Sophie, and told her that she had better not try that again. She said that sometimes she would go to the hamburger place and stand around. If she was lucky someone would buy her some food, or give her their French fries. Her dad just does not care about her, and she misses her mother so much. Then Sophie started to shake and cry. She cried very intensely, and Charlie and Olga did not know what to do. It seemed like she was never going to stop. So Charlie took her on her lap, and rocked her back and forth and told her soothing things, such as how everything would be alright, and that she could stay with them, as long as she liked. Olga did not quite approve of the staying part, as she was wondering how they could afford to feed her. But she did not say anything in front of Sophie.

Charlie did not mind sharing her bed with Sophie; in fact she rather liked it. Once in the night Sophie woke up crying, but Charlie cuddled her and was able to calm her back to sleep without too much difficulty.

The next morning Charlie had to go to work, so Olga had to baby sit Sophie. Surprisingly Olga did not complain. She dug out an old deck of cards, and they played cards most of the day.

Charlie had to tell someone about her ordeal of the previous evening. She did not dare confide in anyone except Betty. So she told her about what happened after Betty dropped her off. Betty was stunned, especially when Charlie told her about how worried she was that she might have killed the brute that was trying to molest Sophie. Then she went on to explain that her and Olga had told Sophie that she could stay with them. Betty asked Charlie, "Can you afford to keep and feed another person?" "Well, come to think about it, Olga could put her down as a dependant when she applies for her old age security and the supplement. That is money she can apply for if her income is low. My grandmother gets it. Are you sure that no one saw you hit that bastard over the head?" To which Charlie replied, "I am positive!" there did not seem to be anyone else around, even though Sophie was yelling at the top of her voice. It was a rather deserted area. Anyway if I had it to do over, I would do exactly the same thing." Betty said, "Then put it out of your mind. Tell yourself that nothing happened and get on with your life." Charlie nodded in assent and thought about how lucky she was to have Betty for a friend.

On her way home from work, Charlie stopped off at a Thrift Store, and bought some clothes for Sophie She did not have any trouble finding some dresses to fit her. Charlie had to resist the temptation to dress her like a boy. But she knew only too well what that was like, so she persevered in helping her to look like the girl she was. Previously with her straggly, long, matted hair, dirty face, and some boy's cast off clothes, it was hard to tell what she was.

When she got home, Charlie got Sophie to sit on a chair while she cut her hair. It was the only way one could deal properly with the matted mess. Sophie was afraid of all this grooming, that she was not used to. But she was happier to have a full belly, and somebody to treat her like she actually existed.

After another shampoo, and a change of clothes, Charlie felt that Sophie had been transformed from a ragamuffin, into a princess. When Sophie looked in the mirror, she stared at herself in amazement. Then she ran to Charlie and flung her arms around her and started to cry. She continued to cry, until Charlie took her on her lap and calmed her down. Sophie kept saying "I want my mommy." Even Olga got tears in her eyes, as she watched the sad little girl. And she vowed inside that she was going to help Sophie as much as she could.

The next morning, Olga took Sophie along with her to the government agent. Olga had come up with some paper work, as if from nowhere. She had a satisfied smile on her face when she left the office. Olga was careful not to expose Sophie to any more people than she had to. So she went right home, and left the shopping for Charlie to do.

The following three weeks went by with much the same routine; of Charlie going to work and Olga babysitting Sophie. Then one day when Charlie came home she was greeted at the door by a beaming Olga, who had obviously been waiting for her return. Olga had a cheque in her hand, and showed Charlie, her first Old Age Security cheque. Charlie was amazed at the amount, and went on to read the letter that came with it. There was an additional amount for Sophie. It caused Charlie to wonder where Olga had got a birth certificate from, but she did not want to ask. So she decided to let sleeping dogs lie. She had never seen Olga as happy as she displayed since Sophie had arrived on the scene. Perhaps it gave Olga a purpose in life now that she was no longer working. For Charlie it was a big improvement in the atmosphere of their home. She did not feel as isolated from Olga as in the past. And Sophie was losing some of her melancholy, crying less for her mother, and even being able to smile once in awhile.

THE PAPER GIRL

CHAPTER SEVEN

Charlie's first upgrading class started the next week. She rode her bike each evening over to the school where they were held. One evening when she was going to ride home, she noticed that her tires were flat. She knew that it was no accident that both tires were flat. An alarm went off in her head, as it was always starting to get dark shortly after her classes ended. If she had to push her bike home it would take awhile and leave her in a vulnerable position. Charlie told herself that instead of getting in a panic, she must do some fast thinking about how to get out of her present situation. She did not know her instructor other than as Mr. Stranahan. She was afraid to strike up a conversation with him, but it seemed the only solution to her dilemma. Since his car was still in the parking lot, she realized that she had better catch him before he left. So she fought back her fears, and went back in to ask him if he would give her a ride home. When she approached him, he looked rather surprised, which only served to heighten Charlie's fear. But she quickly explained to him just what her problem was, and went on to ask him if she could get a ride home? He immediately looked concerned, but was quick to assure her that he would not mind at all giving her a lift home. When they went outside he inspected the tires and said, "It is apparent that someone let the air out of your tires. Some people have a strange sense of humor. I can put your bike in the trunk of my car and we'll stop at the service station and put air in the tires. You will be all ready for riding to work tomorrow morning."

Mr. Stranahan then went on to tell Charlie, that his name was "Rob", and that outside of class she could call him by his first name. So Charlie thanked him for his help and with great trepidation, said "Good night Rob."

Charlie had some home work to do before she went to bed. It took her longer than usual, as she kept thinking about her flat tires, wondering who would do such a thing. She was tired in the morning and had to rush. She was certainly grateful that Rob had seen that her tires had air in them.

The next two evenings of school were uneventful. And Charlie felt more relaxed in class, now that she had conversed with Rob on a more personal basis.

Then it happened again. When Charlie went to get her bike to ride home after class, her tires were flat once more. This time, she found it to be unsettling. Charlie immediately informed Rob about her tires being flat again. He did not know what to make of it. After the other incidence, he had stated to the rest of the class that if someone was playing a practical joke, that it better not happen again. As it put a young lady in a vulnerable position to have to push her bike home after dark, he considered it to be a bad joke. Now he did not think that it was any of her class mates who were involved. Rob did not wait for Charlie to ask for a ride; he quickly assured her that he would give her a lift. The next day was a Saturday, so Charlie rode over to Betty's place to tell her about the bike tire incidents. Betty was just as puzzled as Charlie was.

Betty asked Charlie if she would like to go to the dance the next week end. Of course Charlie jumped at the chance. She missed the fun company of Arnold and Gordon.

She even forgot to worry about her flat tires for a couple days.

THE PAPER GIRL

Her peace of mind was short lived. On Monday when she came out from class, her bike was missing. She searched all around the outside of the building, but to no avail, it had completely disappeared. This time Rob said that he was going to report it to the police. He felt that something strange was going on. When Charlie told Ted about it, he offered to let her use his bike. Charlie wanted to accept the offer in the worst way, but she was afraid that Ted's bike might disappear like hers had.

Charlie finally agreed to borrow Ted's bike in spite of her reservations concerning its safety. Charlie also asked Ted if he had heard from Dave. Ted stated that no one in his family had seen or heard from him for quite some time. So Charlie put the thought of Dave out of her mind.

When Charlie got home from work Olga told her that another woman had been murdered. The police had come and asked Olga whether she knew her, as there was no I.D. on the body. She had also been severely beaten like the old lady that the police thought could be Olga. Since Olga got around a lot they thought that she might have some use full information. Charlie did not tell Olga anything about the bike problems she was having, as she did not want to worry her.

The next time that Charlie rode to class, Rob told her that in light of what had happened with her bike, she could take her bike into the school entry, and park it there. Charlie was very relieved and grateful. She was fed up with bike problems.

Mr. Stranahan gave his upgrading students regular tests as they covered the required material. He was amazed at how Charlie got such good marks. She never had any mark below ninety four.

It was finally near the end of the course, and Rob Stranahan made arrangements for the class to go to the local college to see what further training would be available to them. It was a very interesting, but mind boggling experience for Charlie. She had never known about how many different vocations there were. It was something that she had never spent much time thinking about. But now that her mind had been set on making something more out of her life, she found it rather stressful to consider all the options. Charlie made a lot of notes and collected all the information sheets that were available for them.

A few days later the class wrote their final test, and received an equivalency grade based on their marks. Charlie had achieved a grade twelve certificate. She could hardly believe that she had accomplished so much in just a few weeks of instruction and studying. Charlie rushed home to show Olga her Certificate. Olga looked at the paper several times before she believed it was true. She was so impressed that she got tears in her eyes and actually told Charlie that she was proud of her.

All the talk of education brought about the subject of Sophie going to school. Charlie said that they must register her in a different school than she had attended previously. So Olga said that she would take Sophie and register her for school which would soon be starting, following summer holidays.

Charlie's job at the orphanage gardens would come to an end also at the end of summer. The place would be closed for the winter. Ted and Betty congratulated Charlie for acquiring her certificate. Then they had a discussion about the plans that she and Betty had for the future. Charlie stated that she did not have any money for taking some training in what ever course she might choose. So Ted explained that since her job was coming to an end, she would be eligible for manpower assistance. Betty had forgotten about the assistance, so now both girls were excited. They thanked Ted and said that he deserved to be taken out to dinner. They would not take "no" for an answer and insisted that it had to be that very evening. Besides Ted knew them fairly well, and he might give them some hints as to what career they should choose. Betty took her car, and found a restaurant that was not very crowded, so that they could have a discussion. They thought up every kind of career that came to mind, but they could not get Charlie to choose any one of them. She said that she would have to think things over for a few days before she could make up her mind. So Betty said that she should do some thinking also. They agreed that the girls had to make a decision in one week. Ted said that he would take the girls out for supper if they had both come to a decision by then. Betty told Charlie that she would come over the next day and that they would go to the library to get some help.

When they consulted the librarian, she told them to make a list all the things they liked to do, and then make another list of all the things they hated to do. Then they would discuss what was on the lists and try to come to a conclusion. The girls decided to spend two days making their lists.

At the end of the week Ted told Charlie that something strange had occurred. He went on to say that he had found her bike leaning against his garage wall. There was no clue as to how it got there. Charlie was shocked and confused by the news. It was almost like there was a ghost at work. However Charlie did not believe too heavily in ghosts, as she had never given them much thought prior to the bike incident. So she put it out of her mind.

Two days later, Ted came to talk to Charlie and told her that the mystery of the bike had been partially solved. Ted stated that his dad had been coming home from a late meeting, and had seen the bike leaning against a hedge near his gate. Because it was late, he parked the bike behind the garage, and forgot about it. It would seem that whoever put it near the gate must be knowledgeable concerning the bike's origin.

Charlie was very surprised, but she had decided to put the matter out of her mind, as she had more important things to think about; such as what she was going to decide on for her future education.

When she got home, she found Olga very upset concerning the recent news she had read in the paper. An older lady had been beaten and murdered. It was someone that Olga had known quite well, and had liked because she treated Olga with respect and consideration. Sophie was upset because Olga was upset. So Charlie had her hands full to try to reassure Sophie that everything would be alright. And that it was important for everyone to eat and enjoy their supper. Tomorrow would be a new day and everything would be better.

Charlie was getting concerned about the numerous murders, as the police had not indicated that they had made any progress in their investigations. Charlie had a vivid dream that night. She dreamed that she was running and running for a long time, chasing a figure in black. Whenever she got near him, he would become invisible, and then reappear away ahead of her. Finally he ran off the edge of a cliff and disappeared. Then Charlie woke up. And in the back of her mind she knew what classes she was going to enroll in for starters.

The classes were "Journalism," and "Criminology." And she would find out what else she had to take to become a newspaper reporter. And perhaps later on, she would want to become a detective. A woman detective who would view killers of women from a different perspective than her male counterparts seemed to.

Later on in the day Charlie went to the college to enroll in the classes. She also enrolled in three other classes that were recommended as necessary classes to complete her desires. On her way home Charlie got up the courage to stop in at the Martial

Arts building and signed up for some classes. This was something that she had wanted to do for quite some time. Today she was on a roll. Charlie was very excited about her future studies. She was so excited that she wanted to share it with someone, who would have an appreciation of what she intended to do. So she went to visit Ted whom she loved like her brother, if she had a brother. Of course Ted was just as enthusiastic as she had hoped for. He could not help thinking, and commenting to Charlie how her life was evolving into some very positive future plans. Ted said "I know that you are going to be very busy for the next while, and I won't see much of you, so how about going out for supper with me?" Charlie liked the idea immensely, so they made a date for that evening. Then Charlie hurried home to tell Olga that she would not be home for supper.

The following day was Saturday. So after Charlie did some household duties and the shopping, she decided to go for a run in the park. It was a favorite pastime of hers and she ran for quite a ways. It was starting to get dark as she got three quarters of the way back to the edge of the park. She stopped to take a breather. Then she heard a sound like a kitten mewing, but it was very faint. So she listened for a few minutes to see if she could identify the direction that it was coming from. Finally she heard it again; it seemed to be coming from a few feet to the side of the trail. Charlie searched among some shrubs and then noticed something white. Upon further investigation, she saw a towel that seemed to be covering something. She cautiously lifted the edge of the towel and peered under it. She could hardly believe her eyes. There huddled together within the towel, were two very tiny babies. When she touched them, she could feel that they were very cold. What was she going to do with these two babies? She asked herself. She did not want to be seen carrying them around in a towel. Since she felt that she could not just leave them there, she decided to carry them at least to the edge of the park. As she neared the edge of the park, she saw a police car driving slowly and then stopping. A police officer got out and ran after a man, yelling at him to stop. The man kept right on running and the officer pursued him. There did not seem to be anyone else around, paying any attention to the police car. Charlie immediately saw the solution to her problem. She ran to the police car and put the babies on the seat, then hurriedly walked away. She did not risk waiting until the officer returned to find his new passengers. She knew that if she was spotted, she would have to answer a lot of questions. So she did not waste any time heading for home. This was one incident that she would keep to herself. Of course the next day there was a request for information concerning the babies, both in the newspaper and on the radio

Monday morning Charlie was up early for her first day at college. She was high with anticipation. When she returned home she was loaded with homework. Two nights a week she went to Martial Arts class or worked out at the gym. On weekends she did her share of domestic duties, plus almost an overload of homework.

This more or less set the pace of Charlie's life for the next four years. Olga cared for Sophie and allowed Charlie all the time she needed to complete her studies. Both Charlie and Olga were looking forward to the day that Charlie would graduate. Meanwhile Olga was enjoying her retirement and the care taking of Sophie.

Charlie and Betty saw each other on fairly regular occasions, as they were on the same campus. Betty had decided that she would enter into the world of horticulture. They went out together with Ted once in awhile. And they also went out with Arnold and Gordon, when there was a holiday. Their determi-

THE PAPER GIRL

nation to succeed kept them from getting very emotionally involved with anyone of the opposite sex.

Their social life consisted mainly of an occasional shopping trip.

Ted decided that he didn't want to spend the rest of his life working with plants. So he and his father decided that they would train someone to take Ted's place in the greenhouse. This would free up Ted to pursue the vocation that really interested him.

It was a very disappointed Charlie, when she discovered that Ted had gone away for job training. He wrote her an occasional letter, but wouldn't tell her what his training was for. He wanted to surprise her when he was ready to graduate. He was pursuing a vocation in a field very similar to her interests. In the meantime they both had to be satisfied with a relationship based on mail correspondence.

THE PAPER GIRL

CHAPTER EIGHT

It was a busy morning at the "Daily Herald," the local large newspaper. What with the newsmen and women bustling around, performing the duties related to their part of the daily business of running a newspaper.

Tom Woods, the editor was on the phone talking to his secretary, about the two new people that had been recently hired. As yet Tom had not met them. His secretary had done their interviews, as Tom had been out of town on business. So now Tom was directing her concerning what positions they should be given. He said, "I know that one of them won't like this assignment, but someone has to cover two weddings this weekend. The other one can cover some of the sports, as there is too much for old Hadley to do. So put Patrick on the weddings, and Charlie on the sports assignment." Jane his secretary said, "I think that it might be better to reverse their assignments."

"Just once Jane, could you take a direction without wanting it different," asked Tom. To which Jane smiled to herself and replied, "What ever you say Tom." Then he asked her to have them both report to him later, towards the end of the day. Jane thought "I can hardly wait."

Charlie and Patrick received their assignments. It was the first day for both of them. Patrick accepted his assignment with a long face. Charlie accepted hers with a big smile and a feeling of great anticipation. She immediately set out to find old Hadley. He would be showing her the ropes. When she found him, he did not at first pay attention. That is, until it filtered through to him that his new assistant was a young woman. And she was a really beautiful woman at that. Well, he thought, she won't last long, after a couple days she will be glad to give the job over to a man, someone who can really understand and appreciate sports. Leave it to an old man to underestimate the knowledge and ability of an attractive young woman. Charlie was certainly not a stranger to what went on in the different sports. She had taken part in her share of them while in college and cheered for the other ones. Charlie prided herself on her strong graceful body and her ability in the martial arts. She did regular strength training and liked sports for the workout that she got from them. Physically she was no slouch. Mentally she was keen and alert. Hadley was in for the education that he had missed in life. And Charlie was just the person to do the teaching.

This was the first one on one relationship for Charlie, with an older male. Her older college professors had a more remote relationship. Especially since they were relationships shared with many other students. Charlie had never experienced a father, daughter relationship, since she had never known a father, or even an uncle. Her male parentage was a complete mystery to her. One she had never spent a lot of time thinking about.

At first Charlie was unsure of how she should relate to Hadley, but assumed that since he was in charge, she would just do whatever he directed her to do. She would be careful not to jeopardize her new job in any way.

So Hadley would give Charlie her assignment, and always had the same parting statement; "This is your big chance kid! Knock yourself out!" Charlie liked to interview any player if the opportunity presented itself. She picked up on any humorous or surprising comments. She wrote in a very descriptive and action packed fashion, which really brought the game to life, so that the reader became interested and absorbed in the game. Hadley

THE PAPER GIRL

would comment, "You're doing fine kid, keep it up." As long as Hadley was happy, Charlie was happy.

About two months into her sports reporting, she was working a bit later at the news office. She was putting the finishing touches to her story when a strange man came into the news room. He seemed rather surprised to see her there, and said, "Good evening, may I help you? I am Tom Woods, the editor."

Charlie replied, "Oh I'm glad to meet you, I was just finishing my report for the sports column."

Tom looked puzzled, "I don't get it, and Charlie does the sports column and does a fantastic job."

Charlie said, "We haven't been formally introduced, I'm Charlie Hanson, Hadley has been showing me the ropes." At this point, Tom's mouth dropped open, he paused, and said, but, but, but, I thought Charlie was a man, that is why he got the sports assignment,—well, live and learn. I guess I owe you an apology for assuming that only a man could adequately cover sports and write a suitable column."

Charlie answered, "I guess it's lucky for me that my name is Charlie, I love this job."

Tom said," It seems that everyone is happy, so keep up the good work—Charlie."

Charlie was walking on air as she made her way home. She had to tell Olga how she had shown her boss that a woman was just as good at a job as a man was. Olga nodded and smiled. It was an old story for her.

Approximately a month later, Charlie and her cameraman "Donny", were interviewing some ball players at the end of the field, near the bleachers. They noticed that a disturbance was taking place. Two husky looking fans were harassing a smaller man. They then commenced to holding and hitting him. Charlie was not very far from them, so she told them to stop it and move on, or she would call "Security." Of course Charlie did not look very influential, since she was a slim female figure. So one of them stepped away from his victim and proceeded up to Charlie, laughing and taunting her. Charlie warned him again concerning Security. He laughed and then took a poke at her. Charlie was not to be intimidated, as she had many hours of martial arts training and knew that she could handle whatever he had to offer. In a flash the bully found himself lying on the ground looking up, with a look of surprise and pain on his face. He was sure that he could handle her, so he jumped up and tried to hit Charlie. To his surprise he found himself back on the ground. This time he felt a bit shook up. So he slowly and cautiously got to his feet, and joined his partner. His partner had stopped pounding on his victim, in order to watch what was going on with his buddy. They then beat a hasty retreat from the area, and into the arms of the Security Police. One of the officers asked Charlie if she wanted to press charges. But Charlie asked, "What for? They did not hurt me; it really was nothing to make a fuss about." Donny had it all on film, but Charlie instructed him to cut that part of the film when he developed it. It was to be off the record in their report. She also told Donny to keep quiet about it, as she did not want it to be made public. Charlie then put it out of her mind.

She was glad to get home and shower the dust off, and get a chance to relax. She enjoyed Sophie, who was a loving little girl. She was developing into a clever and entertaining person. Olga's mental and physical health had improved tremendously since her retirement. Because caring for Sophie had given her a purpose in life. She also cooked regular meals, which was a blessing for Charlie, who often worked odd and long hours. They did not have much money but they had harmony and comfort with each other.

THE PAPER GIRL

Two weeks later as Charlie and Donny were finishing up their sports write up, Donny asked Charlie if she would like to come for a beer. He went on to say that every once in a while some of his friends got together to shoot the breeze. They were both men and women, and they enjoyed each other's company. Many of them also worked at the "Herald."

Charlie had never had the experience of drinking beer, but she wanted to fit in with the other staff, so she said yes. There were about a dozen people seated in a rather smoky atmosphere. After ten minutes Charlie longed for fresh air. Introductions were made and Charlie was accepted as one of the bunch. She enjoyed listening to all the stories being spun concerning numerous events, which had occurred over the past year. Donny longed to tell about how Charlie had handled the bullies in the bleachers. But he knew Charlie well enough to keep quiet about it. As the evening drew to a close, Charlie decided that she had enjoyed herself in spite of the smoke she had to breathe in. She thanked Donny for inviting her, and asked if they could not find a place with less smoke.

Donny said that they had never given it much thought, but he had to admit that it made his eyes burn, and probably was unhealthy. And it was especially unhealthy for people like them who did not smoke. Charlie decided that the experience was not worth repeating.

Charlie headed home thinking about all the people she had met, and some of the stories they had told. She had to smile about it all as she got ready for bed. She had her own plans to consider also.

A few weeks had gone by when Tom Woods summoned her to his office. Charlie's first thought was, "what did I do wrong?"

Tom greeted her with a smile and asked her to sit down. Then he said, "Don't look so serious, relax, I have a question to ask you," and then went on to say that he thought that she might like a bit of variety in her work. "The summer sports season is pretty well over. It will be in another week, and then it will be hockey season. I have been contacted by an older reporter who specializes in hockey. But I have to give you first choice."

"How would you like a part time assignment doing some investigative work? I looked over your resume, and it seems that you have the training, to do something more demanding than what you have been doing. Would you like to give it a try? We are really short handed in that area. If things go well, it would become a permanent position."

"You will be an assistant to Rusty. Rusty is rather rough around the edges, but he is very experienced and a really shrewd individual. His nickname is "Crusty Rusty." Just don't feel afraid of him and his unique personality and habits. His bark is much worse than his bite."

At first Charlie was so surprised that she did not know what to say. But this sounded like just what she wanted.

Tom told her that she could have some time to think it over, but that he was rather pressed for time. This brought Charlie to her senses. She eagerly said, "Oh I'd love to try something different, I could start right a way, if you want me to."

Tom had to laugh at her enthusiasm, and told her to come see him the next morning, and he would explain things to her, and get her started.

Charlie was so excited that she had trouble sleeping that night.

The next morning when Charlie attended at Tom's office, she was introduced to Rusty. Her first impression of him was something other than favorable. He had a stubbly beard, of a few days on his face, and his eyes were bloodshot from lack of sleep. His clothes were wrinkled as if he had slept in them several times.

When Tom introduced Charlie to him, He said, "there must be some mistake; I thought that she was here for a job as the new receptionist. You know someone to make the office look nice. I need someone with some substance. Someone I can depend on in a tough situation. Not a pansy that needs pampering and protecting. No, this is not going to work. Besides, I thought Charlie was a man, not a school girl. Sometimes on this job things are not in our favor, and we have to be able to deal with that. We need a lot of grit."

Tom said, "Look here Rusty, she has good qualifications and she can look after herself. Besides I'm the boss and I need someone right away. You have voiced your objections, now get over it. She is your new assistant, and that's the end of the story. Get on with your business and control your negativism."

Poor Charlie would have welcomed an open hole to crawl down. She was too stunned to say anything. And she was anything but delighted to be paired off with this repulsive character. Tom then went on his way after making his proclamation to Rusty.

So Rusty reluctantly told Charlie to follow him down to one of the offices and he would fill her in on what he was presently working on. He had a folder of past notes with pictures and newspaper clippings. And he also had a new folder with the most recent information in it. He told her how he was comparing some old information to some of the more recent events. He was searching for any connection that they might have. He cautioned her that everything in the folders was strictly confidential. That he was seeking out a storey, but at the same time he was working with the police. It was imperative that the public not become aware of any evidence that the police had. Charlie was impressed by how serious the whole business sounded.

Rusty told her that three infants had gone missing from the orphanage. The incidents had occurred over a period of six months. There were very few clues concerning the disappearances. Security had been set up at the orphanage to prevent it from happening again. But the last disappearance had taken place just a week ago.

The babies were all victims of abandonment at birth, and had been placed in the orphanage by Children's Services until they could find homes for them.

Charlie recalled the twins that she had left in the police car, and wondered if they had been involved in the recent situations.

Rusty told Charlie that he would phone her the next morning, when he had decided what they would be doing on the case. Charlie asked Rusty how he was going to phone her, when she did not have a phone. "What do you mean? You don't have a phone?" "I have never needed a phone." Charlie replied. "I have never used a phone."

"Oh, boy! Are we off to a speedy start? I will get Tom's secretary to set you up with a cell phone." Charlie looked alarmed. "I don't know a thing about using a cell phone." Rusty looked disgusted. "Don't worry, I will show you all there is to know about it. You absolutely will need it. I might have to call you on short notice, and you will have to call certain people to get information from time to time. Your job depends on you using your phone, so you better be right on the bit about using it. Many times you will be working against time in certain situations. I have to be able to trust you to come through when it is required. My belief is that if you snooze, you lose. If you think that you can't handle the responsibility, tell me now. Don't waste my time. Keep in mind that I'm not here to hold your hand, nor to wipe your nose."

Charlie tried to remain calm during his tirade; she was beginning to dread working with this bossy character. But she wanted this job, so she would have to persevere. "Don't worry, I can learn the ropes as well as anyone, and I'm not afraid of work, and I'm not going to slack off. I can follow instructions. I trust your knowledge and experience."

"Very well then, I will see you tomorrow morning at nine at Tom's office. Rusty told her. Charlie said, "I will be there." She then made her escape to the stairway. She did not know which was greater, her anticipation of the kind of job she really wanted, or her dread of working with and satisfying Rusty's demands. She realized how backward she must appear to Rusty, when she told him that she had never used a telephone. But it was a part of her life that she took for granted, along with many of the other things that she had missed out on. She did not want to waste time dwelling on things which were beyond her control, and were not really creating a major hardship for her, so she put it out of her mind for the present.

When Charlie got to Tom's office the next day, Tom's secretary called Charlie in. She had a beautiful cell phone for Charlie. It took half an hour of instruction, before Charlie felt confident enough to phone Rusty as a trial call. Rusty was almost at the office when he got the call. He was not in a good mood, so he growled at Charlie, "What the hell are you calling me now for? I am almost at the office." Charlie thought about how he told her not to be late. She figured he was in a bad mood anyway, so she said, "If you were not late, I would not be able to call you, would I? Don't worry; I'm just making a practice call on my cell phone." She heard Rusty swear just as he hung up. She knew that she had not improved his mood, but she had decided that she was not going to fear his moods, but instead she would ignore them. So when he came in, Charlie smiled and said cheerfully, "Good morning Rusty, I'm glad to see you. I bet that we are going to have a great day. Rusty glowered at Charlie and said, "Now are not we little miss, sickeningly cheerful?"

Tom's secretary had to hide a smile, and gave Charlie an approving nod.

Rusty told Charlie if she was ready, they had better get to work. After studying all the information that they had, they came to the conclusion that the disappearances were not random events. They felt that there had to have been some careful planning. And that someone within the orphanage must be involved.

Charlie told Rusty how she used to work at the orphanage, and could probably go under cover as an employee.

Rusty said, "Oh sure you just happen to have worked at the orphanage, don't give me any bullshit stories!" Charlie realized that it did sound convenient, but went on to explain about her and Olga's employment there. Rusty did not bother to apologize for doubting her. Instead he grinned from ear to ear, and said, "Well I will be damned!"

She asked Rusty if the police had done a background check on the staff. Rusty said, "I'm sure that they must have by now. I will phone and ask them to send over what ever information they have."

Charlie said, "After we acquaint ourselves with that information, I will go and see my friend Ted and his dad, about finding a spot for me on night shift. Would not it be exciting if you and I found out who was behind the plot?"

Two days later Charlie went to visit Ted and his dad. Charlie had surprised Ted by phoning him to set up an appointment. They were happy to see her, especially Ted. He was also very surprised, but pleased that Charlie was making progress with her career. He thought back to when he first met her as being a shy, quiet boy. What a change from those days. It was amazing what a beautiful woman she had turned out to be, like a plain drab caterpillar turning into a gorgeous butterfly.

After talking for awhile, it was decided that she could have a job on night shift, doing extra little cleaning jobs and straightening up clothes in cupboards. That would also give her an excuse to go downstairs and check out the laundry staff as well as the cleaning staff. This would give her lots of freedom to move around the orphanage. She hoped to be able to find out something worthwhile. Her employment was to begin the following Monday.

Charlie filled Rusty in on what she had discussed with Ted and his father. Rusty said, "you must be careful not to let anyone suspect that you are there as an investigator. If you compromise the police investigation, we will be in deep do do. And don't you take any foolish chances, as these will be ruthless people that you will be dealing with. It is probably a black marketing ring, selling babies to well to do parents in other towns or in the U.S.

Who knows how extensive their activities might be."

The following day, Rusty was in an angry mood, after talking to the police. There was a new desk Sergeant on duty and he had refused to give Rusty the background information on the orphanage employees. "Not to worry, Charlie told him. "I can get that information from Ted, that way we might get more information about them."

Rusty smiled and said, "You go get the information concerning their names and personal numbers, and I can do some magic with the computer."

So once again Charlie phoned Ted, and asked if he could get the information she needed. Ted did not mind at all. It would give him a chance to see her again. Ted asked, "If I bring the information over to you, will you go to the movies with me, tomorrow evening?" "Certainly, Charlie told him. I will be ready at seven o'clock".

Ted and Charlie had a great time laughing about the movie, and agreed that they should go out more often.

Charlie presented Rusty with the information concerning the employees, the following day. He checked out the addresses and they took a drive around to get an idea of where each one of them lived.

Rusty explained that one can tell a lot about a person from the area that they choose to live in. He told Charlie that he would get the information concerning whether they had any doubtful pasts. He went on to say that he had a friend, a constable in the police force who would get him the information. Ted had not as yet told Charlie that he was a police officer. He still had a month of training before he would graduate from the police academy. He did not want to spoil the surprise. Ted promised to get the information within the next two days.

There were five night time workers at the orphanage. Two worked in janitorial and three in the laundry at night. Three were women and two were men.

After they got back to Rusty's office, he called his friend, to check the police records on the five people. He did not want to wait for Charlie's contact.

There did not seem to be anything significant in the computer information. Except concerning one of the women working in the laundry. She had been suspected of having some involvement in a robbery a few years prior, but nothing had been proven.

Two nights later Charlie went to work at the orphanage. And Rusty started keeping surveillance on the five suspects. After five days Rusty and Charlie met at Rusty's office to compare information. Neither one of them had noticed anything that they could consider as being suspect.

At the orphanage Charlie had learned to her surprise, that there was a baby in the baby ward. She soon discovered that the staff liked to look in on the baby when they had the opportunity. Of course at night the baby was usually sleeping. And there was a night nurse's aid named Ellen, who cared for her. She told Charlie that she would like to have three nights a week off, and wondered if Charlie could relieve her. The baby was very good and slept most of the night, except for a couple bottles. Charlie agreed that if it was alright with the supervisor, that she, Charlie could care for the baby. Ellen assured Charlie that she would fill her in on how to care for little Janie. Charlie decided that when she was caring for Janie, she would not spend much time a way from the ward. She did not want to risk anything going wrong when she was responsible for her care. Charlie asked Ellen if she had worked the night shift before the baby came in. Ellen disclosed that she was called in to work nights whenever a baby came on the ward, and had done so for four years. In the back of Charlie's mind was the thought that she should also have her background checked, even if she had worked there for four years. All the other people who were suspects had also worked at the orphanage for quite a while. The laundry staff had been there the longest. Except for old Barney who had been there for many years and was therefore not considered a suspect.

It was time for Rusty and Charlie to compare notes again. Rusty once again cautioned Charlie to be very careful, as whoever was involved in the other abductions was likely to try again. He told her to go to work early and observe whether anyone carried a packsack or anyway they could conceal a baby. Rusty said that he was going to follow each one home and see if they went right home after work, or if they met with anyone on the way. He could not observe more than one person per morning coming off shift.

Charlie was able to observe the baby from a linen closet if she kept the door slightly ajar. She felt that if it was any of the staff, they would do it shortly before getting off work.

Rusty asked Charlie, "What kind of wheels do you drive?" Charlie replied, "Two wheels." "Don't tell me you drive so fast, that it's always on two wheels." said Rusty Charlie looked disgusted. "I ride a bike." answered Charlie. Rusty started to splutter, "you, you ride a bike? You have got to be kidding. Are you Ahmish? You are the most backward person that I have ever met".

"I'm sorry to be so backward, as you put it, but I have no money to buy a car! My mother and I are poor, and I have a student loan to pay back. I'm doing the best I can. If it's not good enough for you, I will have to quit and let someone else have the job. If anything happens at the orphanage I will phone you right away. At least then you will know who it is."

But life was soon not to be that simple for Charlie. Nothing unusual happened for two more weeks. Rusty was getting restless. He told Charlie that he was going to spend some time cruising around the orphanage grounds. Charlie was restless also, but for a different reason, as she told Rusty. She knew that he would have some disparaging comment about it, but she told him anyway. Usually when it was full moon, as it now was, she had difficulty sleeping. It was from the magnetic pull of the moon. Rusty looked at her with disgust. "Don't tell me your one of those certain crazies that goes loony with the moony." To which Charlie replied "I don't go crazy. But sometimes I sense certain things. I feel that something is going to happen very soon; maybe it will be because of the full moon."

When Charlie went to work everything seemed as usual, that is until around two a.m., when she learned from Pearl from the laundry, that she was suffering with the flu, and would be going home at three a.m.

Then John who washed floors said that he would have to leave because he had the flu.

Then old Barney, who was famous for hardly ever having missed a shift, came early to pick up the garbage. He told Charlie that he had the flu, and was going to leave early. He said that he would go home for a rest and then he would see that the rest of the garbage was taken care of. This was finally the thing that caused the rat to seriously increase the gnawing in her gut. She phoned Rusty and told him, what was occurring. She said, "I don't know who you should watch for. I'm going to the bathroom now; I have been putting it off; because I did not want to leave the baby unattended".

When Charlie got back from the bathroom, she rushed to see that the baby was still there. She looked at the bed twice, as it registered in her mind that the bed was empty. The baby was gone. Charlie almost froze with panic. She could hardly believe that this was happening.

Charlie immediately got on the phone to Rusty. "It has happened," she said in a rushed voice, "the three of them left and then the baby disappeared. John from janitor work left first, then Pearl from laundry, and then old Barney. You try to follow the first two, and I will follow Barney, he likely is not finished loading as yet."

Charlie ran to the laundry, and saw only the other two workers. So she dashed for the back stairs and rushed to the outside, where she came to a sudden halt, when she saw Barney's truck parked down at the end of the building. Charlie stayed in the shadows, up close to the building and tried to be quiet and careful, as she made her way along the building, up to Barney's truck. She could see Barney at an open door, bringing out some bags. Barney threw them onto the back of the truck, and then said, "There; that's the last of them. I will just drive around the corner to the dumpster, and then we can go." Charlie thought that Barney must really be getting old, the way he was talking to himself. When he got into the drivers side, Charlie ran to the back of the truck and jumped on. Barney drove over to the dumpster that was at the far edge of the yard. As soon as he stopped, Charlie jumped off and hid behind a small shed which was beside the dumpsters. Barney opened his door and said, "Come on, you can help me unload, and then we can get out of here more quickly." Charlie was very surprised to realize that Barney had a passenger. She wondered what was going on. Barney was not a suspect up to now. But the facts that he had a passenger, and was in a hurry, certainly were negative indications for his innocence. Charlie thought, "It just goes to show that you can't trust anyone." Nobody got out to give assistance to Barney. Charlie waited for him to finish unloading, and then she sneaked over to the truck and cautiously climbed on and lay down as close to the cab as she could so that she wouldn't be visible. She was glad that it was a dark night. And the yard lights weren't very bright.

Barney left the grounds and headed towards town. When he got near the park, which was on the edge of town, he slowed down. He drove slowly, a little way into the park. There was a car parked by the trail, which went through the park. Barney stopped near the car and got out. So did his passenger. When they got close to the car, Charlie peeked around the corner of the box. His passenger was carrying a pet carrier. He turned just as he got to the car. Charlie had to put her hand over her mouth to keep from gasping out loud. She blinked twice before she could believe her eyes. It was her old friend Dave. He started replying to Barney in a loud voice. "What's your hurry? You'll get your money, after I get mine. Don't you trust me?" To which Barney said, "No I don't trust you, why should I? I have no guarantee that I will ever see you again. You said that you would have a thousand dollars for me as soon as I got you the baby. Now pay up." That was all Charlie needed to hear, she got off the other side of the truck while they were arguing and were intently concentrating on each other. Charlie dashed across to Dave and grabbed the pet carrier, and started to run into the trees. Dave was right at her heels and then grabbing her sweater. So she quickly set the carrier down and came up fighting. She gave Dave the benefit of her martial arts training. She didn't quit until he was only semi- conscious. She took his belt off and tied his hands behind his back and then tied his shoe laces together. She wanted to check on the baby, but she knew that she'd better phone Rusty first. Charlie knew that she had to keep control of the situation until Rusty could get there. But now Barney appeared to be going to give her trouble and she couldn't phone just yet.

Barney had driven up to where Charlie and Dave were fighting. He slowed down, and then got out to help Dave, who was getting beaten; he stopped and then left, after Charlie gave him a well aimed kick. He ran to his truck and stepped on the gas and spun the wheels, and left in a hurry. Charlie was concerned that Barney might come back. But she was more concerned about the welfare of the baby. She took it out of the carrier, where it had started to whimper. The baby did not seem to be harmed, and was likely wet or hungry. So Charlie phoned Rusty. As soon as Rusty heard her voice, he started in. "Where in the hell have you been? Did you lose your phone? "

"I've been wondering, and worried about what's happening with you." Charlie told him to calm down, that everything is under control. She gave him her location and then filled him in on what the present situation was. Rusty spluttered, "There you go again with that bullshit. I will be there in five minutes. Stay put!"

Charlie moved farther back from, and advanced a short distance, from the trail, in case Barney should come back. She also had to stay near enough to where she could keep an eye on Dave. Dave was yelling threats at her now that his head had cleared a bit. Charlie was worried that he might get loose. True to his word Rusty drove up within five minutes, and Charlie took the baby and carrier, and ran out of the trees to his car. "The kidnapper is right over there." Charlie said, after putting the baby in Rusty's car. Rusty gave her a doubtful look, but followed her over to where Dave was sitting and working at his restraint. Now Rusty had an incredulous look on his face. "I'd better call this in right away. This is a crime scene." So Rusty phoned the police. Then he checked Dave's restraint and told him to sit still unless he wanted a clout on the head.

Rusty asked, "Where's Barney? Did he help to tie him up?" asked Rusty, as he pointed at Dave. Charlie said, "For heaven sake Rusty, Barney took the baby and brought it to Dave, who was in Barney's truck, and then they came to the park. I had hidden on the back of the truck. So when they argued about the money, I ran over and grabbed the baby and ran with it to the trees. Dave here tried to grab me, so I used my martial arts training to incapacitate him.

Barney was going to help him, but changed his mind after he tasted my foot. Then Barney drove away. Better phone the police to be on the lookout for him and his truck."

THE PAPER GIRL

Ten minutes later the police arrived, and Rusty told them about Barney. Charlie said that she had to get the baby back to bed, so an officer drove her back to the orphanage and stayed to take her statement. Charlie did not give the officer every detail of their plan and how they carried it out. After all, she reasoned, she and Rusty had to do all the work without very much police assistance. Why should they give away their methods? Rusty phoned her to say that he wanted to talk to her first thing in the morning, as soon as she got off shift at the orphanage. He even offered to pick her up, which she agreed to.

When Rusty arrived to pick her up, he was wearing a big grin on his tired looking face. "Charlie you are something else! He said, "Why did not you tell me about your ability to defend yourself? I was worried sick about you; when you said that you were going to follow Barney, and then I did not get a call for quite awhile. What if Dave would have pulled a gun?" Charlie replied that she took them by surprise, and things happened so quickly that Dave did not have a chance to get a gun. "Besides I figured Barney for a coward. How did you make out following both John and Pearl?"

"Well first John came out and proceeded to toss his cookies, so I concluded that he really was sick. So I waited and followed Pearl. She drove rather slow, and went straight home, so I thought that she must also be sick. That's when I started worrying about what you were involved in. After all I knew that somebody had the baby."

Then Rusty said, "I'm taking you for breakfast, I'm so hungry I could eat a whole pig." Over breakfast they discussed what kind of story they were going to release to the public. Since they did not know who Dave was dealing with, they could not reveal very much. So they decide that they would issue only a brief announcement that would say; Two Daily Herald reporters have rescued a "kidnapped" baby. More details will follow in a later report, as the police have an ongoing investigation into the matter.

When they got to the Herald, Tom was waiting to get the details of their adventure. He was very impressed by the work they had done. He also agreed that they had to be careful about how much information was released to the public. They would have liked to be able to brag a bit, but circumstances would not allow that.

Tom said, "Charlie, this was a trial run for you as an undercover operant. You certainly proved yourself up to the task at hand. Therefore you are now in a higher wage bracket. Rusty thinks that you need more than two wheels, to travel with, so he can help you take care of buying a car."

Later Charlie told Rusty that she does not drive. "Well we can soon fix that, if we get you into a drivers course, in no time you'll be driving. I help you find a good deal on a car. One of my buddies is in car sales."

Charlie was very excited and nervous at the same time, at the thought of being a car owner.

That evening Charlie phoned Ted and arranged to meet with him so that she could fill him in on what was going on with Dave. She hated to hurt Ted's feelings by telling him, just how far Dave had fallen. Ted was as kind and honest as he looked. He had that clean cut, handsome look about him. When she really thought about it, she realized that Ted was much better looking than Dave, who had his lady killer kind of pretty boy looks. Perhaps it was Dave's smooth manners which helped him to bewitch the ladies. Dave certainly did not retain any charm for Charlie after her latest experience with him. Now in her acquired maturity, she wondered how she could ever have found him attractive. Ted was a king, in comparison. Ted was someone who had earned her respect.

Charlie greeted Ted with her usual smile, but felt reluctant to mention Dave. Finally Ted asked, "What's going on with you? Is everything alright? You seem to be holding something back." Charlie swallowed and decided that this was the moment to tell him. She asked, "Ted, have you heard from Dave as yet? You know that Rusty and I have been investigating the kidnapping at the orphanage. Well, I have some bad news. We caught a person snatching the baby from the orphanage, last night".

Ted immediately asked, "How can that be bad news? Isn't that what you wanted to do; Catch the baby snatcher?"

Charlie looked away from Ted and said, "The bad news is—that Dave was that person. He is in jail. Old Barney was his accomplice, but he took off in his truck. The police are looking for him. I am so sorry to have to tell you about Dave's part in this".

It took Ted a minute to digest what Charlie had to say. Then he said, "I'm shocked that Dave would do such a stupid thing. This is going to look bad for my dad, and the staff at the orphanage. It will be a public disgrace.

My mother is going to be really upset about this. She always tried to think the best of Dave."

Charlie assured him that the information would not be given out. The "Paper", would only disclose that the kidnapper had been caught, and that the police are investigating. "They still don't know who is behind the whole business. I am not sure whether Rusty and I will be doing any more work on it or not. If I know Rusty he likely will keep on nosing around."

Charlie went on to tell Ted about how she was going to learn to drive, and with Rusty's assistance she would become a car owner. Ted was pleased for her, and they reminisced and laughed about their bicycle riding experiences.

The following morning, Rusty was all excited about how he was going to find out who Dave was working with. He was also angry at the new police desk Sergeant again. Dave's car had been impounded, along with his cell phone, and what ever else was in his car. And Rusty could not get any information. Other than a rumor that there were no clues left behind by Dave. Charlie thought about whether he could have left any clues at the orphanage, but she could not think of anything. Charlie decided that, she had better tell Rusty about her previous relationship with Dave. Rusty was rather stunned, especially considering how she had overpowered Dave. Perhaps the result of some hidden anger, Rusty thought. Then he asked Charlie if she could think of any way Dave could have done anything to leave a clue behind. It suddenly dawned on Charlie, that Dave might have done something while he was waiting for Barney to empty the garbage off the truck. Dave was a restless character, who had to be constantly moving around. He had a habit of emptying his pockets and discarding papers that he no longer needed. So Charlie was thinking that it was a long shot, but she had better mention it to Rusty. Rusty immediately said, "Let's go, we could get lucky you know." So they hurried out to the orphanage, and searched around the dumpsters. It had been breezy the previous day, so the chances of finding anything were pretty slim. They were just going to give up, when Charlie spotted a small wad of papers stuck up against the fence almost out of sight. The wad consisted of an old motel receipt from a hotel in Seattle, a receipt from a coffee shop, and a gas receipt from a service station in Bellingham Washington.

Rusty was all excited about their good fortune in finding the papers. He asked Charlie if she had ever heard Dave mention anything about any places he had been. She was quick to assure him that Dave never talked about his private or past life. They would have to try to pickup on whatever information that they could glean from the receipts. "Well, Rusty said, I have a feeling that his accomplices are likely in Seattle. But the only way that we can find out is to pay a visit to the places where the receipts came from. How do you feel about a trip to Seattle, with possible stops on the way? We'll have to clear it with Tom first of all." Charlie said, "I can't just up and go to Seattle. I have never been anywhere except to college." "Oh yes you can." Rusty replied, "I'll call Tom right now and if it's a go, I'll drop you off at home and you can pack a bag." So Rusty called Tom and assured him that they had a couple possibly good leads. After some discussion, Tom agreed. "Boy, you can sure be determined and convincing Rusty." Charlie told him, and she had to smile at the smug look on his face. "But I'm still leery about this totally mysterious venture that we are about to embark on."

"Don't worry, you'll be in good hands," Rusty assured her. Then he dropped her off at her house, where she had to convince Olga not to worry, about her trip so far away from home, especially since Rusty had told her to take enough clothes for a week.

CHAPTER NINE

They were planning on leaving very early the next morning. Charlie was so excited that she spent a restless night. However that did not seem to affect her ability to be up at the crack of dawn. She was glad that Rusty was not in his usual cantankerous mood. Now that it was really happening, she was excitedly looking forward to her new adventure, even though she was totally unaware of what was going to transpire.

Rusty drove in silence for awhile and then he told Charlie, "I don't want to scare you, but you have to be prepared that some times when one is nosing around, one might come up against some very unsavory characters. Criminals can be very hard and some are very merciless. That is why I carry a gun. I have a permit for it, and I keep in practice at the shooting range." Charlie paled a bit at this information, but she did not want Rusty to think that she was a coward, so she just looked at him and did not know what to say. So she remained silent, and went on puzzling about what they were going to do first.

As he drove along, Rusty filled Charlie in about some of the previous adventures he had experienced while nosing out some stories. That information did nothing to ease her feeling of getting in over her head.

When they entered Bellingham, they took some gas at the same service station that Dave had purchased gas at. Not far from it was a Mexican food restaurant. Rusty said, "It's been a long time since I had some good Mexican food and my belly button is rubbing my back bone." Charlie said, "I heard that their food is very peppery, and I don't like hot food." Rusty assured her that if they ask for food that is not so hot, they would be obliged. Following their meal, Charlie told Rusty how delicious it was. The taco salad was also something that she could put together herself.

When they got to Seattle, the first thing Rusty did, was to buy a city map at the service station where they bought gas. Rusty said, "I like to keep the top half of the tank full, in case I have to leave somewhere in a hurry. I'm going to study this map this evening, so that I'll know my way around tomorrow. We are going to get a couple rooms closer to the waterfront. After registering at the motel, I am going to pig out on some good, genuine seafood."

Charlie said, "I haven't eaten much seafood, other than some sardines. I guess there are a lot of kinds of fish."

That brought a surprised look to Rusty's face, and then he started to laugh, he muttered the word sardines, and then he laughed even harder. Charlie felt a bit embarrassed at her ignorance of yet another subject. Her hurt feelings must have shown in her facial expression. Rusty apologized for laughing, and went on to detail all the different kinds of seafood that he knew of.

They went to their rooms to freshen up. Rusty had chosen a motel near the one that Dave had stayed in.

They drove to a small restaurant right on the edge of the water. Charlie was delighted, and confused at the variety of choices on the menu. So Rusty ordered two combination plates. They both cleaned their plates. Charlie said that it was even better than Mexican food. When they were leaving the restaurant, Charlie was startled to see a couple rats running around the dumpster. It sounded like a rat convention taking place. Rusty explained that it is very difficult to get rid of rats on the waterfront. He also had a two legged rat in mind.

THE PAPER GIRL

Charlie was glad to get to bed. It took a long time for her go to sleep after her day of new adventures. She did not have any idea of what adventure was in store for her in the near future.

Both Rusty and Charlie were awake early the next morning. They went for breakfast in the small coffee shop near the motel. Rusty had decided that the best way to start their investigation was to go to the motel where Dave had stayed and see if he could get any information. Charlie asked, "Would you like to show them the picture of Dave that I brought along? They might recognize him." Rusty looked surprised, and said, "Good thinking kid, you might make a detective yet." Then he lightly tapped her on the head. Charlie was relieved that she had his approval, at least for the moment.

When they talked to the motel clerk, she did not have any recollection of Dave having stayed there. But Rusty insisted that she check back in their records until she found something. After a few minutes the clerk finally came up with the information. Just then the manager came in and asked her what she was looking for. Rusty told him, and showed him Dave's picture. "Oh yes, that's Doctor Dave, he was not alone, Nurse Kelly was with him as usual. They stay here every once in awhile when Dr. Dave has a customer. He does private adoptions you know. His customers come here to meet up with him, and collect their baby. They are so happy; he does wonderful work for both the babies and the anxious parents. They always say, "God bless you!" "And they really mean it. He meets the prospective parents first, and then leaves to get the baby. But he did not stop back in for a while, he usually comes through a few days later and brings the baby, but he seems to be a bit later this time. In fact Nurse Kelly asked about him yesterday. She was rather worried about not hearing anything from him. She is staying here for a few days until he returns. Would you like to speak to her?"

Rusty quickly said, "No, and I would appreciate it if you did not even mention that we are here asking questions, it would not be fair or kind for us to worry her needlessly." The manager nodded, and made a motion of zipping his mouth.

Just then a woman came downstairs. She smiled at the manager on her way out, and spoke briefly to him. After she left, the manager said, "That was Nurse Kelly. She mentioned that she is still waiting for Dr. Dave."

Rusty told the manager to excuse them as he was in a hurry to get to an appointment. They almost ran out to the street. They looked both ways on the street, but there was no sign of Nurse Kelly. She must have left in a car. Rusty asked the hotel manager what Nurse Kelly's full name was, as she was registered there numerous times. Her name was Kelly Bradley.

They had no alternative but to wait until the next day when she would probably be back to inquire about Dave again. Rusty was as usual thinking about something to eat. But first he wanted to talk to someone from the police department concerning Nurse Kelly's street address. He felt that there must be a faster way to check on her than by waiting to follow her.

At the police department, Rusty had to do a lot of explaining and show his journalist credentials in order to get any information. He finally had to wait for the police to talk to Tom at the newspaper. Tom told them that a police officer was coming to Seattle to assist in the investigation, and that he would get there the next morning. The police finally agreed to give Rusty: Nurse Kelly's address. As soon as he got the address, he forgot about being hungry. He almost ran out to his car, with Charlie rushing along behind him. Once in the car, Charlie started opening the city map and started searching for the street that nurse Kelly lived on. They had to travel numerous blocks before they found the address. It turned out to be on the side of a very large property which hosted a convent. The sign above the gate indicated that it was the Sisters of Purity that were housed there.

Rusty exclaimed, "Well I will be damned they gave us the wrong address." Charlie suggested that they drive around the other side of the property which covered a large area. They looked in astonishment at the sign above that gate. The sign read, "Brothers of Humility". There was a long house like building, with another building behind it, and what looked like several greenhouses.

The Sisters' house was also a very long building with several large rear buildings. There didn't appear to be any movement around either place, as Rusty made another trip around the property. The complete properties covered a whole city block. It was surrounded by a fence and a high hedge.

Rusty said, "There is no point in wasting our time hanging around here. Let's go get some food at that Chinese restaurant I saw a couple of blocks back. We can think about what we are going to do next, while we eat." While they were eating, Charlie reminded Rusty that considering that Nurse Kelly is a crook, she would probably live in an unusual place. She suggested that they wait until almost dark and come back to look around the "Holy Block." Charlie went on to say, "I have a funny feeling about that place, something seems out of kilter, about it." Rusty replied that he would call it women's intuition, and that they had nothing better to go on at the present. So they went back to their motel to wait for a later trip back to the properties.

Charlie had left home in a hurry and had not had time to contact Ted, to tell him of her up coming plans.

She decided that she should give him a call, although he would likely be at work. To her surprise, he answered the phone. She was very happy to hear his voice on the other end of the call.

Ted was equally surprised to get her call. Charlie filled him in on what she and Rusty were doing. After she finished, Ted told her that he felt that it was time for him to present her with the surprise he had been saving for such a long time. However, he said it would have to wait until he got to see her. Charlie felt disappointed that they were in two different places, as she was most anxious to find out what his big secret was. She didn't want to sound like a baby, so she calmly told Ted that she hoped to be able to see him soon. In stead of making her feel better, her phone call had somewhat deflated her enthusiasm. But, she reasoned out that she had to concentrate on the job, and keep her mind on what she must do.

Charlie phoned Rusty in his adjoining room, and suggested that they take a drive over to the motel where Nurse Kelly had been staying. Maybe they would be able to pick up some more information about her. Charlie wondered if the couple who were waiting for Dave to bring their baby, were still around.

When they got to the motel, Rusty asked the manager about the couple who were waiting for a baby.

Rusty asked the manager if it would be alright for him to meet the couple. He said that he and his wife were also looking for a baby to adopt, and that he would appreciate a chance to find out more about it. The manager didn't see why the couple would mind. He said that he would ask them, and told Rusty that their last name was Taylor. The Taylors were agreeable to meet Rusty and Charlie. They came down to the lobby and turned out to be very friendly people from a small town in Montana. Mr. Taylor operated a small garage and service station. He stated that he couldn't afford to wait much longer for Dr. Dave to show up with the baby. He went on to say that the price of adopting the baby was really more than they should be spending. That

THE PAPER GIRL

$20,000.00 was a lot. He had made a deposit of $10,000.00, and was to pay the rest when they got the baby.

Rusty was curious to find out how they had heard of Dr. Dave and Nurse Kelly. Mrs. Taylor said that she had seen the advertisement on the internet, placed there by Nurse Kelly. She had contacted Nurse Kelly, who sent them some literature concerning her good record at doing private adoptions. After all the arrangements were worked out, the Taylors had come to Seattle to pick up their baby.

Charlie could hardly control the urge to tell the couple about Nurse Kelly's scam. But it wasn't the time to do that. They had to get more information, and build a good enough case to put her out of business and be able to prosecute her. So Rusty and Charlie both thanked the Taylors for talking to them and voiced their hopes that Dr. Dave would soon arrive with their baby.

Rusty and Charlie decided that they would wait until almost dusk before they went back to the "Holy Block" as Charlie called it.

When they drove past the Brother's side, they noticed a newly erected sign, which read: Fresh Hothouse Tomatoes. $ .60 per pound. "Well Charlie, so much for your women's intuition. They obviously are making use of the greenhouses. Look there is a Monk by the front of the house attired in his robe. Now are you still suspicious?" Charlie asked Rusty, "Have you ever seen a Monk that young? He is only a teen aged boy. Perhaps he is the son of a Monk." "Very funny Charlie, even I know that Monks don't have sons, at least not where any one would know anything about it. So that means you are still not satisfied." Rusty replied. "It has only served to make me more curious." Charlie stated.

"Let us drive around to the Sister's side, perhaps they will be outside and we will be able to see what they look like."

As they drove slowly around to the back of the monastery, they saw a back gate swinging open. Rusty immediately pulled into a driveway across from the monastery. He shut his lights off, as it was just getting dark enough to use them. Charlie and Rusty watched the gate, and after a couple of minutes, some bicycles appeared from within the grounds. Mounted on the six bikes were what looked like teen aged boys? They all had back packs on their backs. Their bikes were well equipped with lights and reflectors. They proceeded slowly and cautiously at first, peering in every direction before pedaling off to the main street. They then speeded up, each one going in a different direction. Rusty asked Charlie, "Which one should I try to follow? Charlie said, "I don't think it matters, they are probably all up to the same thing, whatever that is."

Rusty tried to follow the bike that he could still see. He had to be careful not to get too close. The cycler didn't waste any time. Rusty had trouble keeping him in sight, and just when he lost sight of him for a couple seconds, he saw the biker wheel into a small park like area. Rusty was fortunate enough to find a parking place just beyond the park. He had no sooner stopped than Charlie was out of the car. Rusty cautioned her to slow down and be quiet and careful, as they sneaked up through the trees surrounding one side of the park.

The boy on the bicycle rode over to a bench where a man was sitting. He handed the man a package out of his back pack. The man gave him something in return. They both took their departure without having uttered a word. The cycler continued up the street, as Rusty and Charlie hurried back to the car. Rusty soon caught sight of the cycler as he turned onto another street. After three blocks the cycler rode up to an apartment building, and soon disappeared inside. Within five minutes he was back on the street, riding away.

Charlie said, "I don't think that we are going to learn much more by following him any farther. Let's go back to the convent, and see what the Ladies of Purity are up to. I would really like to sneak through the gate where the boys came out of." Rusty reminded Charlie that they could get into trouble for trespassing on other people's property.

Charlie, being Charlie did not usually let little technicalities stand in her way if she was really eager to do something. But she did not say anything to Rusty, until they were back at the Convent. They could see what appeared to be the shadows of some one or more moving around in the greenhouses. However the movements were very vague. Charlie asked Rusty to go back to the gate where the boys had come out of. When they stopped, Charlie ran over to the fence. She tried the gate which seemed to be firmly closed and locked. So she went along the fence looking for a break in the trees, where she might be able to see something inside. She finally came to a spot where the hedge had thinned slightly. She was dismayed at what she saw. There appeared to be another fence around everything. The fence was set back in about six feet, and was very high. Charlie groaned in disgust. She thought why can't anything be easy?

Rusty came up beside her, when he saw her pause at the gap in the trees. Rusty just shook his head, as he did not want to make any noise. They both headed back to the car. After they got in and closed the door, Rusty let loose with some very creative language, not fit for a lady's ears. However Charlie did not mind as she felt the same way about it. "Well this is certainly giving us something to think about." Charlie said. Rusty replied, "It has made me hungry, let's go find some good seafood and discuss our next move. It is obvious that some rather strange and probably very illegal activities are taking place on this block. We have to decide what we are going to do about it. How much are we going to tell the police, and when are we going to tell them? I can think better on a full stomach."

After their food came and they had eaten a few bites, Charlie said, "You know that the police are not going to pay any attention to us. We don't have enough information. We have to find a way to investigate just what kinds of activities are taking place in that Holy Block. Also we should try to find out where Nurse Kelly lived prior to coming to Seattle." Rusty replied, "I have been thinking about how we can get through the fences. We need some good wire cutters and pliers. We have to wait until tomorrow evening just after dark. We will have to be very careful or else we will be the ones going to jail. So tomorrow we will pay a visit to the hardware store and the War Surplus store to round up some equipment. I am almost certain that Nurse Kelly is involved in what ever is going on, as she owns the property. It seems like there are several people living there. Nurse Kelly would not have residents there that were not making her a profit in some way."

Charlie said, "We could keep up the pretence of being a couple wanting to adopt a baby. That is one way we could trap her in her black marketing scheme." Rusty agreed that they should go to the Starlite Motel the next morning and make a definite request to Nurse Kelly. "We will ask for a baby boy, and see what she says." Charlie said, "Aw shucks, can't I have a baby girl? Please, pretty please?" Rusty looked disgusted and said, "Never mind giving me a hard time, it's not as if we are going to be parents." Charlie looked at the expression on Rusty's face and then burst out laughing as hard as she could.

Rusty and Charlie were up early the next morning. They discussed the details of the story that they would tell Nurse Kelly. Then they drove to the Starlite Motel and asked the manager to contact her. The manager said that she would be in just before noon if they wished to speak to her. They said that they would be back and then they left. They went to the hardware store for some tools and some good flashlights. There was for them, an anticipation and determination to find out about what was going on at the Holy Block.

Rusty and Charlie met with Nurse Kelly as planned at the motel. Rusty was amazed at the emotional story Charlie had to tell. She even shed a couple tears when mentioning her longing for a baby or even a toddler. Nurse Kelly said that they might have to wait for a while. But she had them fill out some forms which she also signed. She gave them five days to come up with the deposit money. After they left Charlie asked Rusty where the money was coming from. Rusty assured her that Nurse Kelly was going to be out of business before much longer.

Just before dark Rusty and Charlie went back to the Holy Block. They parked across the street and down a ways from the back gate. They watched as the similar looking bicycle riders exited the gate again.

A short time later, they saw the flash of a car light coming from the property, and a cargo van exited through the gate. The two observers were very surprised, and decided to wait a while to see if anyone else was going to leave the property. Each time someone left, they closed and locked the gate. There appeared to be only one person in the van.

After waiting and watching for half an hour Charlie could not contain herself any longer. She had to satisfy her curiosity. So they took their equipment to where Charlie had found the thinning of the hedge. Part of that equipment was a flack jacket for each of them. Rusty had been adamant that they wear them, just in case of some unexpected events which they might encounter. They then proceeded to quietly snip some wires until they had a hole large enough to crawl through. They then cautiously proceeded a short distance along the inner fence before they cut another hole. They felt that the holes would be less noticeable that way. As soon as they were through the second fence, it was obvious that some activity was going on. The area around the greenhouses and sheds was unlit. There was a lot of movement within one of the greenhouses. It was not possible to see into the long sheds. Rusty and Charlie were closer to the greenhouses than to the other buildings, so they stayed very low and then crawled on the ground as they neared an entrance. Charlie carefully opened a flap which covered the opening at one end. She quickly closed it again, as she saw a person moving around inside. The unmistakable strong skunk like smell of marijuana permeated the air. They observed that there were six greenhouses in all. Rusty whispered to Charlie to move back from the greenhouse. They crawled back, part way to the shelter of a small shed. Rusty said, "We have to be very alert and quiet if we expect to look in one of those sheds."

They proceeded very slowly, crawling most of the way, pausing every few feet to rest and watch for guards. When they got near the closest long shed, they could hear voices. They were raised in anger. It sounded like some boys were having a lively disagreement. One voice yelled out, "You are so damn lazy; you work like a sick snail. I have to work twice as fast, or else we will not have this shipment ready. I am also fed up with the careless way you handle those chemicals, one of these days you will cause us all to be blown to kingdom come. Kelly should have left you in Iowa to fend for yourself. We are darn lucky that she gave us a job and a place to live!" The other by replied, "Oh yea we are so lucky, we have to work like slaves, we have no more rights or freedoms than slaves. Kelly is making a killing selling this stuff, and we don't get much more than something to eat. I do not believe her story about how things are going to get so much better for us. She is a cold, heartless, greedy bitch." The other boy yelled, "You come outside and say that, you are getting the other boys worked up, causing them to be dissatisfied. You are a born trouble maker."

Suddenly the door burst open and the two boys came hurtling out, Charlie and Rusty jumped back, too late to go undetected by the boys who had come out to fight. One of them sounded the alarm, and Rusty and Charlie ran for the fence as fast as they could. One of the boys tried to tackle Charlie, but she throat punched him, knocked him to the ground and kept on running after Rusty. They were through the first hole and headed for the second one, when a shot rang out. Rusty dropped like a stone. The lighting was very poor, so it was virtually impossible for the shooter to tell if Rusty was dead or not. Charlie was at Rusty's side like a flash. He moaned and swore briefly, then jumped up and they ran for the last hole that they had cut in the fence, and were out. Just then two more shots rang out and Charlie paused in mid step. She managed to keep going as Rusty pulled her along to the car, opened the door and pushed her in. Rusty almost feinted at the sight that Charlie portrayed. Her head was covered with blood and there was blood still flowing profusely. Rusty called 911 and then spun gravel until he turned the corner. He then put a jacket around Charlie's head and tried to stop the bleeding. Charlie was unconscious and did not feel the pressure that he applied. Rusty saw the ambulance coming, and did not waste any time pulling up to it and jumping out and yelling, "Over here, over here!" The paramedics put Charlie in the ambulance and headed for the hospital with Rusty close behind. Rusty was saying his prayers like he had never said them before. He was shaking like a leaf and felt sick to the stomach. He thought If Charlie dies I will never be able to stand to live with myself. Suddenly Rusty heard the scream of police cars.

Because of the shots being fired, someone had called the police. Rusty called them to tell them what was happening, and what the exact location was. When Rusty called in, and identified himself, he was surprised to have Ted come on the line. Ted told him that he had been sent down to Seattle from British Columbia, as the officer working on the kidnapping case. Rusty said, "I did not know that you are a police officer, Charlie did not say anything." "That is because she does not know. It was going to be my surprise for her, so don't you tell her." Rusty paused and then said, "Oh, I won't tell her." Rusty then went on to tell Ted that it seemed like there was a grow operation and likely a methamphetamine lab on the Holy Block, which was represented as being a convent and a monastery. I imagine that you will be preparing a raid on that setup. The property is registered to our dear Nurse Kelly. Ted wanted to know what was happening about Nurse Kelly and her black marketing of babies. Rusty told Ted about the plan that he and Rusty had to pose as adoptive parents. That they were waiting for Nurse Kelly to find a baby for them. In the meantime they were investigating her. Rusty did not tell Ted that he was calling from the hospital, and that Charlie had been shot. Ted said, "I had better get back to things, I will call you later and we can hook up. I am really looking forward to seeing Charlie." Rusty flinched at Ted's words but could not tell him anything about Charlie being injured until he knew more about it himself.

Rusty was desperate to know what Charlie's condition was. The nurse on duty told him that Charlie had been taken from emergency into surgery. The only thing that they could do was to wait until the surgeon was finished. Rusty was in agony, but he had no choice except to wait. The nurse told him that there was a coffee vending machine at the end of the hall. It seemed to Rusty that hours passed before the surgeon appeared. In reality it had been nearly two hours. The surgeon said that Charlie was in intensive care, and would be asleep for quite a while. She had lost a lot of blood and would be very weak for some time. She had been shot in an area of her head that did not sustain much damage other than to leave some bone fragments which they had to remove. There was no damage to her brain or facial features. She would be short of some hair for awhile. The surgeon considered her to be very fortunate that the bullet had only grazed her skull. He noted that it was also fortunate that she had been wearing a flack jacket, as she had also been hit in the back of her shoulder. This reminded Rusty that he had also been hit, and he now realized that the area was very tender. Fortunately he had been hit on his flack jacket. But it had left a nasty painful bruise. He had been so worried about Charlie that he had forgotten all about his own injury. The doctor told him to go home and get some rest, as Charlie would not wake up for hours. So Rusty went to his motel and took some pain killers. He went to bed and dozed until Ted phoned. Rusty knew that he had to tell Ted about Charlie. So he asked Ted to come to the motel. Ted could stay in Charlie's room for the night. But first Rusty had the unpleasant task of telling Ted the complete story. When Rusty finally got to the part of the shooting episode, Ted was greatly shocked. He wanted to go straight to the hospital. Rusty had to do some fast talking to assure him that it would be a useless trip and that they should wait until morning. They talked for quite awhile and then Ted agreed to spend the rest of the night in Charlie's room.

Ted was up early the next morning and called Rusty, who did not have a restful sleep. His bullet bruise had pained, and had kept him tossing and turning most of the night. They both agreed that the best way to start the day was by having a good breakfast.

Rusty volunteered to remain at Charlie's bedside for the day. Ted did not have a choice. He had to go to work. Following breakfast, they did not waste any time getting to the hospital. However they met with disappointment, when the nurse told them that Charlie was still unconscious. She was in a cooled room, as she had started to run a temperature. The nurse explained that her elevated temperature was likely a side affect of the jarring of her brain. All this information only served to make Ted and Rusty feel more worried and helpless. Ted had to leave for work and Rusty stayed at the hospital, waiting for an improvement in Charlie's condition. About noon Ted phoned Rusty to inquire about Charlie. He told Ted that the police were bringing in a Swat team to carry out a raid that night on the Holy Block. He planned to come to the hospital right after work. Rusty was wishing that he would get some good news concerning Charlie, but every thing seemed the same. The nurse told Rusty that he looked like hell, and that he should go home, take a nap, and come back later. Rusty was relieved that she had made that decision for him.

Rusty did not wake up until he heard pounding on the door. It was Ted who had gone to the hospital on his way home. He was told that there was no change in Charlie's condition, so he decided to come home and take Rusty out for supper. Rusty directed him to his favorite seafood place by the ocean.

Ted told Rusty that he would like to be in on the raid that was planned for the night, but he had not been included. He asked Rusty if he would like to come with him to watch from the next street over. Rusty was bursting with curiosity about what they were going to find on the property when they raided it. So after dark they drove over to the place that they hoped to observe the maneuver from. It was very quiet around the Holy Block. There was a patrol car stationed all day on each side of the property. It seemed that no one was moving around. Silently four cars surrounded the property. Then suddenly numerous vehicles of uniformed Swat members closed in on the buildings. And the sound of orders being called out could be heard. There was lots of commotion around the greenhouses. And people were being led out and put into three vans which had arrived. The vans drove quickly away with what appeared to be a lot of very youthful looking boys. Then they heard some yelling of orders, which sounded to Rusty like they were at the long methamphetamine building. There were more orders being called out, a short silence, and then a couple shots fired. All of a sudden a loud explosion was heard and felt, followed by a scream. Flames started leaping into the sky. Rusty and Ted were startled by the jolt and both cursed at the same time. Shakily Rusty had put the car in gear and moved over to another street. The force of the blast had moved Rusty's car sideways. Ted commented that it must have broken a lot of windows in the surrounding neighborhood. Two minutes later the fire truck and ambulance sirens could be heard screaming in unison as they quickly neared the fire. Ted said, "I hope that there were not many injuries to the troopers. It is a shame that they have to lose a life or limb because of greedy, corrupt people. I had better go over and see if I can be of any help."

But when Ted got to the scene, they would not let him in, even when he showed his badge. He was told that it was because of security reasons they were not letting anyone in who had not been screened previously. So Rusty and Ted decided to leave and drive over to the hospital to see how Charlie was. They were directed to a ward, where Charlie had been moved to. The nurse told them that she was no longer running an elevated temperature. However she still had not woke up. They were both shocked at how white her face was under the white head bandage. The nurse said that it was due to blood loss, but that her face would be much pinker in a couple days. The nurse said that no one knew just when she would wake up. She said that it could be in an hour or in a week. She said that it was alright to talk to her even though she gave no response. Ted sat by the bed and held Charlie's hand. Rusty noted the tears in his eyes and decided that he would go and get some coffee. Ted talked to Charlie about how sorry he was that he had let her get into such dangerous situations. That he would never want anything to hurt her. How she is the most precious thing in the world to him. How he was certain that he could not go on without her in his life. He promised her that from now on he would see that they stayed close to one another. "Please, please wake up Charlie and give me one of your beautiful smiles. I have missed you so much for a long time, and I have been thinking about how wonderful it would be if I could take you in my arms, and hold you close to my heart." Then Ted leaned over and very tenderly, kissed her on the lips. He sat back, and tried to control his sorrow, as he knew that Rusty would be coming back. Rusty arrived a couple minutes later, bearing two cups of coffee. They drank their coffee and made small talk for a few minutes, until they heard some movement in Charlie's bed and then a couple of moans. Rusty quickly went to summon the nurse. It seemed that maybe Charlie was waking up. The nurse said that they could remain if they were very quiet, as she did not know how Charlie would react to being awake. Charlie did a lot of moaning and made struggling motions for a couple minutes. Then she opened her eyes and looked cautiously around the room. Finally she asked the nurse, "Where am I? What is going on? Why am I here in this bed? Why does my head hurt? Who are you? I am scared, really scared and tears appeared in her eyes. Will you help me? You look like you will help me? Please?" The nurse reassured her that she was alright and that she was taking care of her and that there was nothing to be afraid of. The nurse said "You have two friends who have come to see you, to see that you are alright. They are right here and would you like to see them?" Charlie quickly replied, "I do not have any friends here, I do not know you and I do not know what your name is." "My name is Nancy," replied the nurse, "What is your name?" Charlie thought for almost a minute, and then said, "I do not know what my name is. Why do I not know my name?"

The nurse said, "You have had a bump on the head, and sometimes people lose their memory right after that happens. It will likely be better soon. Maybe by tomorrow you will remember your name. Would you like to meet the two people who were worried about you and came to see you?" Charlie said, "I guess it would be alright. You won't go away will you Nancy?" to which question Nancy assured her that she would stay right there with her.

Ted and Rusty did not know what to think of Charlie's apprehension. When Nancy asked them to come and say hello to Charlie, and they came over to her bedside, she gave no indication of knowing who they were. She politely said hello to each of them, as Nancy told her their names. Charlie said, "It is nice to get two new friends even if I do not know who I am."

This statement, made by Charlie caused Rusty's face to turn pale and caused Ted's face to become even paler. They stood as if frozen and barely managed to tell Charlie hello and that they hoped that she would feel better tomorrow. Rusty was the first to regain his composure, so he said, "I guess that you are not feeling very strong yet. So how would it be if we left now and came back tomorrow when you will be feeling better? Charlie smiled and said, "That would be nice." Rusty and Ted made their exit. Rusty could see that Ted was very upset. Ted said,

"This is terrible and certainly not something that I had expected or even considered that Charlie would lose her memory. I feel so powerless, not knowing what the future holds for her." Rusty replied, "It is not really all that bad. If she doesn't remember you, you can get to know each other all over again. The outcome will be the same as far as what kind of relationship will transpire between the two of you. You know the old mutual attraction thing." Ted looked at Rusty and asked, "How do you know so much? I have never seen you with any female. I got the impression from Charlie that you are rather sour on women and tend to thus be a bit sarcastic. However your behavior does not seem to faze Charlie. She just overlooks it and actually likes you a lot. She laughs and says that your bark is much worse than your bite. She is wise for someone who has never owned a dog." Rusty had to smile at Ted's comments. Then he contributed that he had experienced several serious disappointments in his life time that probably have a very negative affect on how he deals with people. He added, "It is the way that Charlie accepts my behavior, that makes me feel that she is a very special person. She has strong and definite opinions about what she considers to be a common sense issue. She lets me know in no uncertain terms, just what she expects of me. However I am afraid that she has learned some of my flowery vocabulary to use in those instances, and does not hesitate to use it." The two men conversed some more about Charlie as Ted drove to the police station. Rusty appreciated that he was able to tag along with Ted and keep up with the events of the case.

When Ted reported at the station he did not get much information about the raid. He did learn that no one had seen Nurse Kelly. Rusty had a suggestion for Ted. He said, "I know that Nurse Kelly came from Iowa, why don't we try to get some more information about that, and take a drive out that way? It will take your mind off Charlie, and maybe given a bit more time, her memory will improve. Maybe the officers got some information from the boys that they took into custody. There must be some connection between those young boys and Nurse Kelly. Since Charlie is not able to meet with Nurse Kelly at the present in our plot to trap her, we may as well look for some other information. Ted replied, "I think that before I drive anywhere I am going to question those boys one by one. Maybe one of them will tell me something. I am going to spend all day interviewing the boys. I will give you what ever information you need for writing your newspaper story. You may as well go and see how Charlie is, and try to jog her memory."

So Rusty drove around the city for awhile and then went back to the hospital. The doctor had just visited Charlie. The nurse at the desk told Rusty that the doctor was ready to release her, as her wound was healing nicely, and she could function just as well if she went home and took things easy for awhile. When Rusty went to Charlie's room, she was upset and confused about leaving the hospital. Rusty assured her that she had a room at the motel and that he would take good care of her. He explained about Ted having to go to work.

After Charlie was settled down in her motel room, Rusty filled her in on their background. He explained to her how it was her job to help him write a story about the activities of Nurse Kelly. He said that he was hoping that she would soon get her memory back. But that she should not panic about it. He went on to tell her about what a good report writer she was. His words seemed to calm her down.

When Ted came back after work, he was very pleasantly surprised to see Charlie there. They went for supper at a nearby restaurant, as Ted did not want to tire Charlie. Ted kept smiling all through the meal. Rusty said, "You act like the cat that drank the cream, what is going on?" Ted replied that he would enlighten them after supper, as he had discovered some interesting information concerning the boys and Nurse Kelly.

They settled down in Charlie's room and Ted filled Rusty and Charlie in on what he had learned. He had written the information and names down for future reference. It seemed that Nurse Kelly had been the wife of a religious cult leader in Iowa. When he decided to take another wife, a mere child of twelve, Kelly decided to leave. Kelly had some relatives in Utah who were involved in other polygamist organizations. In the Iowa cult, it was the females who were important and were used as sex slaves. Therefore there were young boys who were pushed out to fend for themselves. They had little education and no job training. So Nurse Kelly devised a plan whereby she gave them a home in exchange for their obedience and work.

In the Utah communes the boys were also victims of sexual abuse. Some of them from the time they were still babies. Kelly was able to rescue some of those boys as well. Of course the boys were grateful to Kelly for getting them out of their unpleasant circum stances. They were not aware of her ulterior motives for rescuing them, or that she was involved in several crimes. They were unfortunates, just looking for some security. Nobody likes to go hungry.

Charlie was beginning to get brief flashes about past events in her life. They were very brief and only served to add to her confusion. She decided not to mention any thing to Ted or Rusty until she could get a clearer image of some particular event. She was beginning to realize that Ted seemed to be very fond of her and she started to wonder what kind of relationship they had in the past. However she did not want to run the risk of asking the wrong questions, so she kept her silence. Charlie was feeling much better to the point of being bored. She felt like getting some real exercise. So she looked in the phone book for a fitness center and got some information. Then she asked Rusty to take her there. Rusty was very surprised that she had come up with that particular idea. When he questioned her about it she could not find any answers, except that she felt that she had to go. So Rusty took her to the center for the next four days. It was on the fourth day that she realized that she had martial arts training. There was a martial arts class going on in the attached gymnasium, and Charlie seemed to just gravitate towards it. Then she got a very strong urge to take part in the competition. The instructor was impressed by her ability. But Charlie was still too weak to maintain her usual endurance, and felt it necessary to explain why she could only tolerate a small amount of activity. The instructor invited her to come back whenever she felt like it. Charlie thanked him and said that she would be back the next day for another brief session, as she had to gradually regain her strength. Too much activity still brought on a head ache.

Charlie slept like a log and woke up in the morning feeling very rested. After she sat up and looked around her room, she suddenly felt overwhelmed. She started to remember who she was and why she was there. Memories flooded her mind, and she had to lie back and try to make sense out of the many things that she was remembering. She recalled that Rusty and she were doing an investigation for a story, and that she was waiting for Ted to arrive. She had been looking forward to seeing Ted again as she had really missed him. But how come he is a policeman? The last thing that she could remember about Ted was when he taught her to ride a bicycle. And after that a few phone calls. Perhaps tomorrow she would remember more things from the past.

Rusty took her to the gym again for the next three days. Ted was gone most of the time, working on the investigation of Nurse Kelly's illegal projects. Charlie was remembering a lot about her past, but not letting anyone know about it.

Then Ted came home with startling news. Nurse Kelly's body had been found in a car, which had been parked in a remote area on the edge of the city. Someone had beaten her and then stabbed her. There weren't any clues as to who had committed the murder. Ted said that this seemed to be the finale on his part of the investigation. He would likely be heading back home in a couple more days.

Rusty asked, "Charlie, are you ready to help me write this article for the newspaper? Has your memory improved? Charlie wanted to tease him a bit, so she said, "I can't remember anything. You are going to have to write the whole article yourself. Rusty got a disgusted look on his face and said, "Oh no, after all we have been through and I am left holding the bag? This is too much! " Then he swore a few times. Rusty's face quickly turned red and he apologized for not being more sympathetic concerning her condition. He reminded Charlie of a whipped dog, and she actually felt sorry for him.

Charlie started to laugh, and then she had to laugh really hard when Rusty glared at her and said, "Are you nuts? I do not see anything funny about this crappy situation." Charlie felt that she better let him off the hook, so she stopped laughing long enough to look over at Ted and ask, "Ted, do you remember how I was a boy and then became a girl, and how you taught me to ride a bike? And how Old Barney kidnapped the baby from the orphanage? What has happened to Dave? Rusty looked very surprised and said, "Thank God! You can remember!" Ted's face was beaming with joy. He said, "It is such a big relief to know that you are remembering things. Do you remember that I had a surprise for you? I was not a policeman the last time you saw me, and so telling you was to be my surprise and I was planning on enjoying that moment of surprise. Some things just do not work out the way we plan."

Ted got such a sad look on his face that Charlie felt sorry for him and said, "I am really surprised, and it is especially surprising that we ended up together working on the same case. But more than that, I am happy to be with you, now that I remember how much I missed seeing you. It will be great to get back home also. Olga is probably wondering what happened to me."

Rusty said. "I will start looking through my notes today and check to see if we need to gather any more information while we are here. If we do not, then we could head back home tomorrow. Is that alright with you Ted?" "I will be completing my paperwork today," Ted replied, "And then I will also be ready to leave. I guess we can plan for an early morning start?" Charlie and Rusty both nodded their heads in agreement.

Everyone was up early the next morning, and ready to get on the road. Of course Rusty had to have his big breakfast first, so everyone went to his favorite place. Rusty rubbed his belly and said, "I am sure going to miss all these good eating places." Ted and Charlie laughed. Then Ted asked Charlie if she would ride home with him. He stated that he had something important to discuss with her. Charlie was only too happy to oblige.

Ted and Charlie left early in the morning to start their journey back home. Rusty was going to come later, as he said that he had a few things to do before he could leave. Ted guessed that it was either the breakfast place or the waitress. The way Rusty ate, it was surprising that he was skinny.

Charlie and Ted spent the day talking about all the things that had occurred in their separate lives while they were apart. They did a lot of empathizing with each other over any negative aspect of their experiences. Their relationship was not dissimilar to an engine which gradually became warmer and warmer as it purred along. They decided to buy a take out lunch and find a private place to park. They were both tired of eating in restaurants. They had found a very pleasant quiet place to park. So after finishing their lunch they were not in a hurry to leave. Ted felt very unsure of himself with Charlie, so he asked her if he could put his arm around her. Charlie was very pleasantly surprised and quickly said, "I would like that." Ted put his arm around Charlie and hugged her tightly. An electric jolt shot through Charlie's body. Ted could also feel the magic and he kissed her briefly, then again with great intensity as his emotions began their release from all the restraint he had been exercising for many days.

As for Charlie, she had never felt this way before in her life. She was on cloud nine and hanging onto Ted as tight as she could. Her lips were begging for more. Ted released her long enough to tell her how much he loved her. He was telling her how beautiful and wonderful she was. Charlie was soaking it up like a sponge. She felt like pinching herself to see if this was all really happening. When Ted paused for a second, Charlie finally spoke up. "Oh Ted I did not realize that I felt this way about you, that I love you so much. It is like being in heaven holding you like this. How are we ever going to be able to stop hugging long enough to drive home?"

Charlie's question brought Ted to the realization that it was time to resume their journey. So with great reluctance they continued on their way with Charlie sitting as close to Ted as she could get.

It was early evening when they got back to their home town. Since they were both very hungry, they went to a restaurant for supper. They were also very tired and strung up with emotions, so Ted took Charlie home and they agree to meet the next day.

THE PAPER GIRL

The next day arrived before Charlie was ready for it .She was still tired from the previous day. But when she came wide awake she recalled her latest moments with Ted. And a warm glow encompassed her being. She carried out her morning toilet and ate her breakfast, all in a state of dreaminess. When Ted phoned she was filled with anticipation at the very thought of talking to him. Her hopes of seeing him were soon dashed when Ted explained how he had been called out for another job. There had been a murder over night, and he was assigned to the case.

A short time later Tom phoned Charlie to come into the office, as he had a new assignment for her. He said that she would have to get started without Rusty, who was coming home that evening. Tom apologized for not giving her more time at home before she had to go back to work. But he stated that the criminals do not give any one time off. Charlie was getting a hopeful feeling that she might be working with Ted once more.

While Charlie was getting ready to go to work, Sophie came to talk to her. Sophie was very shy and rather hesitant to speak. But Charlie encouraged her to tell her what had been going on in her life with Olga. Sophie looked concerned as she told Charlie that she had become aware of the fact that Olga had been going out at night after Sophie was in bed. She stated that she just could not think of a reason for Olga's actions, and that she was very worried about what might happen to her. Lately Olga had been talking a lot about an old friend of hers named Lucy. It was someone that she had known for many years.

Since Charlie did not have much time to talk to Sophie, she said that she would talk to her that evening after she got home from work. Now Charlie also had some questions spinning around in her head. Why did Olga do these worrisome things?

When Charlie got to the newspaper office, Tom was on a coffee break. So she went to the office that she shared with

Rusty. There was a rather fat looking file lying on Rusty's desk, with a note on it. The note said, "Charlie please read!"

Charlie stood and looked down at the file for a few seconds. Then she walked over and gazed out the window. Charlie was not ready to get down to business. She was busy thinking about her conversation with Sophie. Charlie was very concerned about what Olga was up to. Why would she go out at night? Charlie was aware of just how secretive Olga could be about her thoughts and actions. But she was also aware of how old her mother was and that she probably was not very able to defend herself if she came up against some undesirable character.

Charlie came to the conclusion that thinking about the matter was not doing any good, and that she had better get that new file read. So she reluctantly returned to her desk and opened the cover.

The first page had a title that grabbed Charlie's immediate attention. "Disappearing Women"

Charlie went on to read that the women were all old women. She wondered why anyone would be bothered about old women. They wouldn't likely be a threat to anyone. Charlie thought, first we have disappearing babies, now we have disappearing grandmothers. She could see the reasoning behind the baby issue, but the old lady case seemed rather redundant. Charlie recalled the time when the police came to check on Olga after some older women had been attacked. Perhaps there was a connection somewhere. Charlie spent a couple hours studying the file. Then she went to the police station to get some information about the instances of old ladies being assaulted. Charlie encountered a lot more files than she had planned on. Many of the cases were about spousal abuse. Charlie made only brief notes about those cases and then put them aside. It was more likely that the crimes were committed by some serial perpetrator. She spent the rest of the day reading files.

When Charlie got home she was starving hungry. Olga had made supper and smiled so affectionately at Charlie that Charlie did not want to spoil the meal by bringing up any serious or unpleasant topics. Sophie looked relieved when Charlie winked at her and made small talk as they ate. After they finished supper and the cleanup was completed, Charlie asked Olga if she could have a talk with her. Olga agreed in a rather hesitant fashion, she had a wary look on her face.

Sophie had left quickly to go to her room to do her school assignment.

Charlie got right to the point with Olga. She said, "Haven't you noticed that Sophie is upset about something? Don't you think that she is aware of the things that go on around her?"

Olga shrugged her shoulders and put a very innocent look on her face. Charlie looked and sounded very firm as she said to Olga, "Do not try to play any games with me. I want to know why you have been going out at night, and I want to know what is going on with you. I want the whole storey, with none of your lies, like you used to hand me when I was a kid. I have this really bad feeling that you are up to something bigger than you can handle."

"Sophie mentioned that you have been talking about your old friend Lucy" Charlie paused when she saw Olga's face suddenly go very pale. Olga lowered her gaze and remained silent.

Charlie waited for Olga to give some kind of reply. Olga looked up and there were tears running down her face. With a trembling, low voice she said, "I am afraid that Lucy is dead, I haven't been able to find her for two days and nights. She didn't show up for our last meeting and I can not find any trace of her. She had planned to give me more details this time. Last time she gave me the key and said that she had much more to tell me this time. I am afraid that she might have been found out and has had something bad happen to her."

Charlie was so surprised that she stared at Olga in disbelief. She finally found her voice as the cogs in her head were spinning around. "What are you talking about mother? What was Lucy getting information about? Why were you helping her? You could also be in danger if she was."

Olga replied in a slow voice, "I never told anyone, not even you, that Lucy is a private detective. She has been doing under cover work for the police for years. Lately she has been trying to get as much information as she can, concerning the murders of the elderly women. It is really a dangerous position for her because she is elderly and could easily be chosen as a victim. But on the other hand, who would ever suspect her of doing an investigation for the police? The reason I am helping her is because she needs some one to look out for her, some one she can depend on, plus people are used to seeing us together. She needs a contact to help her if she gets into trouble. It just seemed logical that I should be her contact as well as her buddy." Charlie did not want to disclose to Olga that she had been assigned by the newspaper to search out the story concerning the murders. So she began asking Olga a lot of questions concerning the information that Lucy had given her. She asked Olga to show her the key, and asked if she knew what it was for. Olga told her as much as she could recall at the moment. She did not know the purpose for the key. Charlie recognized the key as one that would likely be used in a bank security box. Olga said, "Lucy said that she had an idea as to who the killer is, but that she would tell me a lot more this last time when we were supposed to meet. She said that many of the murders are the work of a serial killer. And that her suspect has friends or relatives in high places. She said that his situation in life has helped him to remain invisible." Charlie told Olga that she must stay in that night. Olga immediately became very upset. So Charlie told her that she would phone Ted and ask him what to do. Then the thought struck her mind that Rusty might be home. So she called Rusty on his cell phone. Rusty answered on the second ring, and Charlie breathed a sigh of relief. At first Rusty found all this information a bit difficult to put into perspective. But when he comprehended that this was the new case that they were assigned to work on, he said, "I am coming right over there and talk to Olga myself, as this sounds really interesting and probably greatly helpful to us."

Charlie just had time to make some coffee before Rusty was knocking on the door. Charlie opened the door after checking to see who it was. She thought, this is getting to me already and we haven't even made a start on this case. Rusty seemed very happy to see her, but he looked rather tired. So Charlie apologized for getting him out at night and expressed her appreciation for his coming over. When Olga saw Rusty she started to ask him to help look for Lucy. Rusty asked her if she knew where to look. He pointed out to her that there was not much use driving around uselessly. He had to have a lot more information before he could even consider trying to find her. Charlie said that she had been studying the reports all afternoon, but had nothing in particular to relate to Lucy being involved. Olga's information threw a whole new perspective for her to consider. Then Charlie showed Rusty the key that Lucy had given Olga. Rusty asked Olga if she knew which bank Lucy banked at. Olga said that she was pretty sure that Lucy used more than one bank. Rusty asked, "Do you know where she lives? Have you been there today?" To which Olga replied, "Of course I know where she lives, she has not been there for nearly three days." "Then does she have a cabin or cottage at the lake or somewhere that she might hide out?" asked Rusty. "Did you hang out with her in any particular place?" Olga said that lately they had been meeting after dark and going to Lucy's house with out showing any lights because Lucy was worried that Olga might be targeted if she was seen with Lucy. Lucy had been quite uneasy about things after she thought that she had a prime suspect. She had not reported it to the police as yet because she wanted to be sure that she was not mistaken.

Rusty said that he must get home and get some sleep so that he could get up early to read the police file. He assured Olga that they would do their best to find Lucy, but that in the meantime she had to stay at home and be careful. Charlie agreed to meet him at seven in the morning at the office. She said that when ten o'clock rolled around she would be trying all the banks to see where the key fitted.

The next morning Charlie ate her breakfast in a hurry. She could not get to the office fast enough. Rusty was already there when she arrived. They spent three hours reading and discussing the information. Charlie made notes as they read through the many pages. They looked for similarities in the reports of several murders. Charlie told Rusty about three other files she had read concerning physical abuse of old ladies. She thought that there could be a connection. After ten o'clock Charlie started going to the first bank on her list. She proceeded to try every bank, but the key did not belong to any of them. Charlie went back to tell Rusty about her fruitless search. Rusty said, "What is our next town that has a bank? Let's try there."

Charlie suggested that they pick Olga up and take her along. Charlie felt that Olga was likely going stir crazy just sitting and waiting. Olga asked if they could drive past Lucy's house, which was situated on the edge of town, and was on their way to Chase, the next town. Rusty drove past Lucy's house and then around

THE PAPER GIRL

the back street, but there was no movement any where. Rusty stated, "We do not want to draw attention to ourselves. Where is Lucy's car? She must have driven it somewhere. I will come back at night and search Lucy's house. I might find a clue concerning where she might be."

They continued on to Chase to try the bank key. Soon after entering town, Olga sat upright and said in an excited voice, "There is Lucy's car parked by that old building. Let's get out and look at it." Rusty said, "No way! We are just going to drive by with out drawing attention to ourselves. We don't know who might be watching and the car could have been put there as bait for someone looking for Lucy. We can not be too careful." When they tried the key at the bank it did not belong there either. Rusty stated, We seem to be batting zero, so lets go on to the next town, that key has to fit somewhere! But first I am going to the town office and find out who owns the building where Lucy's car is sitting." Rusty came back to the car saying "I got a name, which at this point does not mean much, so lets keep on to Salmon Arm."

Salmon Arm has several banks. Rusty said, "I am starving lets get some lunch, and I'll pick up a town map. It will save a lot of time if we know where we are going." It took the rest of the afternoon to check out the banks. At the last one, when they were feeling discouraged at their fruitless search, they finally hit pay dirt. The bank was just going to close and the teller did not want to open a safety deposit box. Fortunately Lucy had named Olga as a person who could have access to the box.

Charlie had brought a case to put the box's contents into. They would look at the contents when they got home. It seemed like the longest car ride that they had ever endured, as they were all so curious about what Lucy had left for Olga to read. Olga fell asleep on the way home in spite of her excitement. It made

Charlie realize once again that Olga was starting to feel her age. She had experienced a hard life and it was taking its toll on her. She should be sleeping at night, not rendezvousing with Lucy, and now worrying about her.

When they got home Charlie pulled out the envelopes that had been in the safety deposit box. The envelopes were numbered. So Charlie handed envelope number one to Olga to open. It was a letter from Lucy. Olga did not feel up to reading it, so Charlie read it out loud for everyone to listen to.

The letter started out; "Dear, dear friend; stop worrying about me! I am fine! The last time that I saw you I was not sure whether I would ever see you again. The police had arranged for me to go into a witness protection program as soon as things looked bad for me. I knew who to watch for and I was to meet with him, the appointment was a danger signal to me that he had figured out that I was onto his identity as the killer. I made the appointment to meet with him, the following evening that you and I were meeting. This gave me a chance to protect myself. Instead of meeting with you I contacted Corporal Scott of the "Special Unit", and he helped me to do my disappearing act. I know that it is hard for you to be sure that I am safe, but some time you can ask Corporal Scott as to whether I am safe. The "Unit" has taken care of selling my property and I will be given a house and car at my new home. I have to make a new life for myself. The hardest part will be to stop working and have time on my hands to miss my old friends. We old people don't seem to have much trouble making new friends. It is easy to get involved in some volunteer work. And so this is good bye old friend. I have left you an envelope with the information concerning the evidence that I collected. Do not contact the police chief as it is his grandson who is the murderer. I have known Chief Rubin for many years. His first wife died after Jerry, their one child had married. Jerry is also a cop and a workaholic. He spent a lot of time away from home taking extra assignments.

When Jerry had been married for two years and had a one year old son, Jerry's wife left him and the child behind, and she ran off with a smooth talking character from some other province. Bill Rubin had remarried the year after his first wife died. Jerry had no one to look after his son Earl, and was too cheap to pay anyone. The childcare job went to Carrie, Bill's new wife. Carrie was a big loud woman who did not like children. This was apparent to the neighbors, but no one could get through to Bill or Jerry that little Earl was being mentally and physically abused. Everyone wondered what had possessed Bill Rubin to marry such a tyrant. It seemed that their common sense was on vacation when it came to the child's place in life. And so another bigger crime was committed by them, than any crime they had ever worked on. I babysat little Earl a few times right after Jerry's wife left. He was the sweetest, cutest little boy that anyone could ask for. It really upset me that he was so afraid of Carrie. He hung onto me and did not want me to leave him with her. When I mentioned it to Jerry he just passed it off as Earl being homesick for his mother. The pain of the whole situation troubled my heart, but my hands were tied. I had heard about how Bill Rubin had penalized some people who had made negative comments about Carrie. Nobody liked her, but Bill could not admit that he had used poor judgment when he married her. And so she went on to ruin the life of a beautiful child. When Earl was about ten years old, I heard a rumor about how he had killed his cat. He had beaten the mother cat to death with a baseball bat because he felt that she was too nasty to her kittens. This always stuck in the back of my mind. So when the evidence started pointing to someone with Earl's background, someone with a lot of built up anger and not much love, it did not take long to fill in the spaces.

I am not sure about where Earl is residing or what he does for a living. I lost track of him after he ran away from home when he was only fifteen or sixteen years old. I expect that Carrie must be high on his hit list, since she was the one who was so cruel to him. He might blame me for not rescuing him when he was little, besides fearing the information that I might have gathered about the murders.

I have all the evidence documented that I was able to come up with, and it is in envelope number "two". Be very careful about what you do with it. Do not let Bill Rubin know about it.

Envelope number "three," is strictly for you and Charlie. Do you remember how we discussed buying a house together after I retired from this case? I have saved my money for many years and am in a position to buy that house now. However "fate" has dealt the cards as a different hand than I had intended for my life to play out. I have been given a house and a car and I have some money with me. You will find enough money in that envelope to buy a nice house for you and Charlie. It is two hundred thousand dollars in one thousand dollar bills. Deposit it into a savings account until you are ready to buy the house. Olga, your days, of living in old shacks is over. I can assure you that I am enjoying being able to give this money as much as you will enjoy your new home!" It was signed, "With all my love, Lucy"

Rusty let out a big sigh, like he had been holding his breath. Then he exclaimed, "Wow! This is incredible!" Charlie said, "Yes it is almost overwhelming; what are we going to do with all this money? I am afraid of being robbed." Rusty replied, "I am going to call Tom, hopefully he is still at the office. We will put the envelopes in Tom's safe. It will make us all feel more at ease to know that everything is secure." "That's a great idea Rusty. I am glad that you are here." Charlie said with a sigh of relief.

So they were soon at the newspaper office and Rusty carried the package to Tom's office while Olga and Charlie waited in the car. After Rusty took them home, Olga went right to bed, as she was emotionally and physically spent from her day's experience. Charlie and Rusty planned to be in the office early the next morning and were looking forward to a very interesting day.

The following morning Charlie had just finished making coffee, when there was a knock on the door. Charlie glanced towards the window and saw a police car outside, so she opened the door without checking to see who it was. When she opened the door a pair of arms grabbed her and hugged her so tight she could hardly breathe. Then she was being kissed on every part of her face and neck. A man's voice was softly calling her all sorts of endearments. Charlie was so surprised and happy that she did not consider resisting. She finally found her voice and said, "I am so surprised and glad to see you Ted, and I love your greeting. I hope that you are going to be home for awhile." Ted was grinning from ear to ear as he replied, "I am going to be around for awhile I hope, but you are going to spend the day with me, no matter what your boss says." Charlie looked very serious as she told him that she was going to work in a few minutes. Then she said, "You can come along, you will be very surprised about, and interested in what we are working on. I have many things to tell you, and they all hinge on unexpected good luck." Charlie refused to give Ted any details until they arrived at the newspaper office. Rusty showed up at approximately the same time. Then Charlie and Rusty filled Ted in on the details that they knew thus far. Ted was astounded that they had lucked into Lucy's findings and that she had passed the information on to them. So they headed to Tom's office to get the envelope and to discuss with Tom concerning their plans. Tom was still trying to grasp the fact that Rusty and Charlie were in possession of a lot of information. He felt that the next thing to do was to go through it and try to match it up with what there were in the files that they had. He had put in a call to Corporal Scott of the Special Unit, asking to come to the newspaper to meet with them. Tom could not tell him what the meeting was about, but that it was a high priority for them to meet. So Corporal Scott was meeting Tom early in the afternoon. Meanwhile Rusty told Charlie to copy the sheets of information and put them in the safe. He wanted to make sure that they would be able to have a storey, once the police had made their case.

Corporal Scott was shocked to realize who Lucy said the killer was. Having to investigate and charge the grandson of the police chief was hitting a little to close to home. Ted said that he knew Bill's son, Jerry Rubin slightly, but had not worked with him. Corporal Scott warned them to be careful and let the Special Unit police handle things from here on. He said that they would be putting surveillance on Chief Bill Rubin's house and his spouse. They all agreed that that was the best way to deal with the matter as they only wanted a storey, not to become heroes.

Charlie wanted to go to the bank and deposit the envelope of money into Olga's very small savings account. So she took the envelope and got Ted to go with her, as she felt nervous carrying all that money around by her self. After they deposited the money they went back to Charlie's house. She had a lot to tell Ted concerning what they planned to do with the money. Olga was relieved to know that the money was safe. She told Charlie how she was so happy to be able to move from the shack of a house that they now lived in.

Charlie asked Ted if he would be able to help her and Olga to find a house to buy. The realtor would show them houses but they would like Ted's input concerning quality and location.

Ted said that he would be happy to help them, that he would find it an interesting fun thing to do. They planned to start looking within a couple days, as soon as the realtor could set up some appointments. In the meantime Rusty and Charlie had to go through all the police files and the information that Lucy had given them. Ted planned on helping them since it was part of his job, to have the facts of the case.

As they poured through and compared notes, it soon became clear to them that Lucy had been much more observant and had followed many small clues that the police had not picked up on. She was also very astute about what and how certain clues were connected. Lucy had an above average ability to problem solve. She was also totally unbiased about who was guilty of what. The reading, comparing and note making was very time consuming. They were still at it ten days later. In the meantime Charlie, Olga, and Ted were viewing houses in the evening and on weekends.

It was Sunday evening, and Sophie and Olga had retired to bed. Ted and Charlie were sitting on Charlie's beat up old couch. Ted said, "Charlie, we do not seem to ever have any time to ourselves." At this comment Charlie sat as close to Ted as she could and reached her arms up around his neck and pulled his head down so that his lips were close to hers. The next thing she knew Ted was kissing her in a very intense fashion. Charlie was kissing him back with all the fervor of her pent up emotions which she had kept in check for too many days. They were whispering endearments and holding each other as close as they could. Then Ted broke away long enough to ask Charlie if he could ask her something important. "Charlie," he said, "Since we have been looking at houses, I think that I would like to contribute some cash, and we could buy a better house. That is, what I am trying say is, will you marry me?" Charlie replied,

"I would have to really think about that, as it was not on my agenda." Ted got such a surprised and hurt look on his face that Charlie quickly said, "I am teasing you, of course I would love to marry you." And she proceeded to show him just how much she loved him.

After several minutes Ted said, "I would like to set that wedding date for not too far into the future. Wouldn't you?" Charlie replied, "I will have to think it over and figure out what would be a reasonable length of time to finish up some things, and then I will ask you about whether that amount of time is suitable to you also." Ted agreed, but warned her that he might prompt her if he did not get a definite answer fairly soon. He kissed her good night and went home, a happy man. Charlie was so happy and excited that she could hardly sleep that night.

The next day when Rusty and Charlie were discussing the murder investigation, they asked Ted if the police knew the whereabouts of Lucy's suspect. Ted said that they did not seem to think that Lucy was absolutely accurate in her analysis of who the killer is. Ted felt that they wanted to get more evidence because her suspect was related to the Chief of police.

Charlie did not speak about what her feelings were about the matter, but she figured that if it was old men that were being murdered instead of old ladies there would be more police action in the case. She asked Rusty who owned the old building where they had seen Lucy's car parked. Rusty said, "It belongs to a James E. Rubin. That must be a relative of Bill Rubin. But it doesn't tell us where Earl Rubin is. I heard that Earl moved around a lot, that he had a job as some kind of salesman." Charlie said, "You would think that they would be quietly investigating his whereabouts, and his activities." Charlie could not get the thought of that building out of her mind. She felt that it was some how involved in the whole business of the murders.

THE PAPER GIRL

The next day when they got to work, they were told that Carrie Rubin, Chief Bill Rubin's wife was missing. She had not come home last night. In fact she had been gone since the previous morning. The police were looking for her, but did not want Tom or any of his media to make it known to the public. Charlie and Rusty both, almost in unison, said to Ted, "I bet she is going to turn up dead. Lucy knew what she was doing and who the killer is!" Ted said, "It is about a month since the last murder of an old lady." Charlie observed that it was also a full moon. Rusty looked at Ted and winked; Charlie saw him and stuck her tongue out at Rusty. The men burst out laughing. Charlie decided to ignore them, as she left for home.

After Charlie got home from work she made a decision to drive to the next town and look around that old looking building where Lucy's car had been parked. She knew that the men would not approve of her actions, but she felt drawn, as if by a giant magnet. She made sure that she had her good flashlight and her cell phone, also a pry bar. She was going to see what was inside that building. There must be a clue there. At the last minute she decided that she had better leave a note for Olga telling her where she went, just in case she got into trouble.

When Charlie got to her destination and looked at the front of the building it looked very ordinary. There was no activity. But since she was there, she decided to go around the back and see what it looked like. There was a door, almost hidden by old rose and grape vines. There were a couple windows, but they were high above the door. It was impossible to look in. Charlie listened by the door for a few minutes. She could not hear anything, so she tried the door. It did not open. It had an old time door lock. So she got out her skeleton keys that Rusty had given her. She tried one that usually opened the old time locks. To her surprise the door opened easily and soundlessly. As if someone had opened that door lately. Charlie paused and listened before she opened the door any wider. Then she opened it and stepped quickly inside before she could change her mind. She held her breath and stood very still. The place had a very nauseating odor about it. It was getting dark outside, so that made the interior shadowy. Charlie was in a small entrance room. She could see that there were rooms beyond where she was standing. There did not appear to be any one around, so she went into the next room which was a large room with a few pieces of furniture in it. Charlie took a couple steps into the room. The floor creaked and she ducked down behind a large stuffed chair near at hand. There were two doors across from her, on the other side of the room. Each one of them stood slightly ajar. Charlie was barely breathing as she had a creepy feeling running up her spine. Then she jumped when she heard a loud moan come from behind the left door. The sound tapered off into a long low moaning. Charlie could feel the hair stand up on the back of her neck. She was thankful that she had taken cover behind the chair. The moaning was mingled in with some mumbling and crying. Charlie wondered if she should chance going to the aid of the person who seemed to be in a great deal of pain. But caution held her back. She felt like covering her ears so that she wouldn't have to listen to the constant agony of that person. The moans were suddenly punctuated by a scream. Then Charlie heard a taunting voice asking, "Aren't you enjoying this you old tyrant? You sure used to enjoy inflicting pain on me. Now the shoe is on the other foot! I have waited for years to be able to pay you back for all the beatings, and the way you made me feel; like I did not have a right to be on this earth. You made my life a pure hell!" There was another scream followed by a loud moan. "You fooled my dopey dad and my conceited, dense grandfather. But worst of all you destroyed my world. I shed an ocean of tears crying myself to sleep every night. My heart was absolutely broken. I felt so lost when my mother left me. I felt like I had no one to love me and hold me close. My dad was off in his own world. Then you came along and I thought, "I am so glad that I will have someone to at least hug me once in awhile. But you soon showed me what a hallucination that was. You! With your loud, sneering, bossy voice! You! With your big mean hands, not to mention those big cruel feet that you used to kick me until my ribs felt like they were breaking. There was a sharp scream as the voice asked, "How do you like to be with out any hands and feet?"

"I have come across a few other old tyrants like you and I thought about how their grandchildren must feel. And I decided that there are too many people like you in the world. So now your turn has finally come to get a taste of what real pain is all about. You are the last one on my list. When you are gone, I will be satisfied. I will be cleansed from your cruelty."

The screaming and moaning were more than Charlie could stay and listen to. She came out from behind the chair and rushed to the door into the entrance. She was just in the process of opening the outside door, when a large good looking young man appeared almost beside her. He wore a very blood stained apron and was carrying a bloody knife. Charlie panicked for a second, feeling doomed after the things she had just heard. She was so terrified that she paused for a second, but then suddenly remembered her skills, and kicked the knife out his hand followed by a swift spin to give him a kick to the groin. As he crumpled in pain she gave him a solid kick to his head. Charlie was out the door like a flash and ran for the safety of her car, just as a speeding police car pulled up and stopped in a cloud of dust, as the brakes were applied. Ted and Rusty jumped out of the car. Ted had his gun drawn and yelled, "Stop! Get on the ground!" The man was not running fast as his groin injury had slowed him down, but he was getting close to Charlie. Ted feared for her safety and repeated his order. The man stopped, and Ted proceeded to run up to him and put the cuffs on him. Meanwhile Rusty was holding onto Charlie whose legs had collapsed under her once she had reached the car. Charlie was as white as a sheet and her teeth were chattering as she said, "You have to call an ambulance, there is a dying woman in there. I did not see her, but I heard her screaming and moaning." Ted put his prisoner into the police car and called for back up, and for the ambulance. Rusty insisted that Charlie had to show him where the woman was. She did not want to go back into the house, but she wanted to help the poor suffering woman. She told Rusty, "I am pretty sure that it is Carrie Rubin as he was talking to her about her meanness to him when he was a boy. The sounds indicated that she must be in bad shape." When they entered the house they could not hear anything. Rusty opened the door to the room and they both gasped with horror. The woman was almost naked and totally covered in blood. There were a lot of cuts on various parts of her body. It appeared that she might have passed out, as she was very still. The room was permeated by the smell of both fresh and old blood. There were a lot of old blood stains on the walls and floor. The paramedics arrived and were shocked at what they saw. They hurried to get the patient onto the stretcher and on her way to the hospital. From their initial findings and observation of the amount of blood loss, they felt that her chances of recovery were very slim.

Rusty and Charlie were joined by Ted, whose backup had arrived. Ted phoned Cpl. Scott of the Special Unit and told him what had transpired. Someone would have to break the news to Police Chief Bill Rubin and to Constable Jerry Rubin concerning Carrie's demise. Everything was in Cpl Scott's hands now. Ted said, "He wants us to stay here until he can get here. Let's take a quick look around without touching anything, as forensics will likely be here before long, as well as the Cpl. "They did not spend much time in the building, but preferred to wait in the car as they discussed the night's events. Ted refrained from scolding Charlie, but Rusty did not. He asked, "Charlie just what processed you to do such a crazy, dangerous thing, as to go to a strange place alone without any gun or backup?" Charlie replied, "I did not think that I was going to find much of anything. I was just going to snoop around. I was curious about this building ever since we saw Lucy's car sitting here. It just stuck in my mind." Ted said, "I am just glad that you are alright, but you can be sure that we will be discussing this later. I think that we have all had enough for one night and will appreciate the sight of our beds."

Ted knew from experience that Charlie would be finding it difficult to put that bloody sight out of her mind. He knew that she would have nightmares and experience difficulty sleeping that night. So he did not want to compound her problems by making her feel any worse.

When Cpl. Scott arrived, he was very excited and started by congratulating Ted on apprehending the perpetrator. He was anxious to view the crime scene, but his grasp of just what had occurred there soon changed his upbeat mood. He said that it was the most shocking incident in his career, as it was evidently the scene of several tortures and murders.

The next few days were a whirl of activity at the newspaper. Rusty and Charlie were working on the rare, sensational story. They heard that Chief Rubin had resigned as Police Chief and was unavailable to anyone. At the end of the week Tom called them to his office to discuss the story. He told them that as soon as they had the story wrapped up, they would be getting two weeks off. He stated, "You have earned it, and need to take a break from all this unpleasant business. By the way, a little bird told me that a Police commendation is in the offing for your good work in breaking this long running case."

It took Rusty and Charlie a couple days to complete their work. Charlie asked Rusty what he was going to do with his days off. Rusty replied that he was going to go to Hawaii and lie around, and eat all the seafood that he could find. Charlie said, "Rusty, I have a favor to ask of you. Ted asked me to marry him, and of course being of at least a bit sound of mind, I said yes. Since I don't have a father, I was wondering, that is, I would really appreciate it if you would give me away at my wedding." Rusty looked somewhat surprised, but after a brief hesitation, he went over to Charlie, gave her a big hug, and said, "Nothing would give me more pleasure. When is the big event?" Charlie replied, "We have not been able to decide that just yet, but it will likely be fairly soon. So have a good holiday and phone me when you get back."

Charlie knew that she, Olga and Ted would be looking at houses and making a choice while they had the time off. She was anxious to get every thing necessary done to clear the way for her new life with Ted. Her life had taken on new meaning and she could not live it fast enough.

On their first day off from work, Ted and Charlie had breakfast together. They were very excited about discussing some wedding plans. Charlie told Ted that although she did not know his sister, she would like her to be a bridesmaid. She planned to meet her friend Betty for lunch that week and ask her to be her bridesmaid for sure. It was an agreement they had made years earlier that they would be one another's maid of honor.

Ted said that he was going to ask two of his fellow officers to be the best men. They planned until nearly noon, and then Charlie realized that she had forgotten about telling Olga that

Ted had asked her to marry him. So they went to tell Olga about their plans.

Three days later the house hunters found what they considered to be their dream house. It was on the edge of town, situated on an acre of land. There were a couple of large out buildings, and because the house had been owned for one year, there was a lot of finishing work that had been completed. The vendor had moved away, and so they were able to get it at a good price. There was a separate living area for Olga and Sophie. And a school bus went right past their gate. They could have possession of the house at the end of the month. This meant that Charlie and Olga would move in before the wedding. But before any one did any moving they had to buy some furniture and household necessities. Ted said that the first thing he was going to do was to install a security system. There had been a lot of home invasions recently. The offences included thefts and sexual assaults.

Charlie's time off work seemed to end much too soon considering the number of things she had going on. Rusty had returned from his holiday looking tanned and rested. Charlie told him that he looked ten years younger. Rusty was his usual self and told her to "Cut the bull."

There were several stories for them to work on at the newspaper. "Crime never takes a rest and the public never tire of reading about it" observed Rusty as they each chose a different problem to concentrate on.

Ted and Charlie decided that they would get married in six weeks time. They were planning on a small wedding with immediate family and a few friends. There was not time or money for a big blow out.

Olga was relieved that she did not have to be very involved. She was still upset about her friend Lucy being out of her life.

Sophie was occupied with school activities. But she was secretly extremely excited about being Charlie's flower girl at the wedding.

It seemed to Charlie that getting ready for a small wedding, coupled with moving, was almost more than she could handle. She shuddered at the thought of the preparation that went into a large wedding, especially considering it was completely for a one day event.

Ted and Charlie had to do some shopping every day in order to buy the furnishings that they wanted. When everything had been moved in, Charlie wandered through the house, savoring the sight of her new home. It all seemed like a beautiful dream; an unexpected stylish new home, and soon a new husband to share it with. It would take some getting used to after the previous places she had called home. Of course she would have been happy to share the old shaky house, as long as it was with Ted.

Finally every thing was set for the wedding day. It started with a beautiful blue sky and loads of sunshine.

Everyone showed up on time and the ceremony and celebration were as wonderful as the weather.

Ted made a special toast to his bride. He stated, "Charlie, my dearest, we have had many interesting adventures together, and I know that you will see that we have many more. You started out in my life as a Paperboy and now look at you! Here is my toast; "To you Charlie! The Paperboy who became a Papergirl! To My Papergirl!" Everyone laughed and raised their glass.

THE PAPER GIRL

EPILOGUE

Two years have passed since the wedding day of Ted and Charlie.

It is the end of a nice sunny day, in which Charlie and Ted had taken advantage of the nice day by doing some planting. They waited until the sun was low in the west and the air had cooled somewhat. Their project was to add some flowers to the front yard. When the job was complete they went to sit on the patio and relax. Charlie was the first to speak. "I am glad that we finally finished planting mother's favorite flowers. Do you think that she is watching and is pleased? It is sad that she never really had much time to appreciate her nice home. She spent almost her whole life living in old dumps and wondering where our next meal was coming from. It doesn't seem fair that she died so soon after she finally bought her own home."

Ted said "Look at the bright side of it. We are fortunate enough to be able to benefit from her friendship with Lucy. Perhaps Lucy will return now that the murderer of all those women has been caught. But maybe Lucy's destiny will forever remain a mystery to us." Charlie replied, "Of course you are right, we are lucky, and we have Sophie to think about. She will soon be graduating from Junior High. She went over to visit her friend Nancy. They're all excited and making big plans for what ever girls make plans for on these occasions."

Ted was quiet and thoughtful looking for a brief time, and then he said, "I feel that perhaps we should adopt Sophie, so that she would have a more secure feeling about life in general. What do you think about that?"

Charlie looked a bit surprised at first, and then she smiled and said, "That is a very good idea, and thank you for being so kind and considerate. It is no wonder that I love you so much. She will be staying over night with Nancy, so that means that tomorrow would be a good day to tell her."

"Tomorrow we will tell her that we would like her to be part of a family. Our family! Now let's go to bed so that we can get up early. Tomorrow is the start of a new day and some new adventures." Ted laughed and said, "Yes we have lots of those, and we benefit from them all!"

Made in the USA